City of Stories Home

Spread the Word
The Albany
Douglas Way
London
SE8 4AG

Design by Franek Wardyński
Franekwardynski.com

ISBN 978-1-9998254-3-0

Contents

Foreword

City of Stories Home celebrates libraries as places to make and share stories, engaging writers and readers from across the capital and the importance of libraries as places of community and connection. This powerful collection of diverse stories on the theme of home is the culmination of that work, representing a snapshot of the great writing that the project inspired.

Delivered by London's writer development agency Spread the Word, in partnership with London Libraries, City of Stories Home celebrates London's libraries, invites writers and aspiring writers to tell their own stories about home inspired by our commissioned writers'—Natasha Brown, Caleb Azumah Nelson, Amer Anwar and Jarred McGinnis—own stories, and London's readers to discover new stories reflective of the communities in which we live and work.

Throughout February 2022, over 700 people took part in 33 free online creative writing workshops hosted by every London library service, with sessions being led by our City of Stories Home emerging writers Iqbal Hussain, S. Niroshini, Ruth Goldsmith and Lizzie Damilola Blackburn and writer-facilitators: Maame Blue, Tice Cin, Jemilea Wisdom-Baako, Helen Bowell, Lorraine Brown, Arun Das, Charlotte Heather, Annie Hayter, Shagufta K Iqbal, Amita Murray, Carinya Sharples and Chris Simpson.

Workshop participants were invited to enter their work to our 2022 City of Stories Home 500 word story competition with an amazing 300 entries being received. The judges, our commissioned writers, had the tough task of whittling this down to a winner and highly commended writer from each participating borough.

This anthology brings you those winning and highly commended stories, alongside new writing by our commissioned writers Natasha Brown, Caleb Azumah Nelson, Amer Anwar and Jarred McGinnis and our emerging writers Iqbal Hussain, S. Niroshini, Ruth Goldsmith and Lizzie Damilola Blackburn.

The anthology takes you on a journey across London—starting in the North, moving through Central and the East then South and finishing in West London. The stories reveal a multiplicity of voices and responses to the theme of home—as vibrant, complex and energetic as London is itself.

Congratulations and thank you to all the winning and highly commended writers; and to you, the reader, enjoy travelling on a literary journey across London, guided by over 60 talented writers, inspired by a workshop they'd undertaken with their local library.

Ruth Harrison
Director, Spread the Word
June 2022

#CityOfStoriesHome
spreadtheword.org.uk

North London

BARNET
Ruthie Raphael: Taking the Tablets
Shereen Pandit: Collateral Damage

ENFIELD
Pamela Kandekore: House-Proud
Lisa Hardy: Africa My Ancestral Home

HARINGEY
Aisha Phoenix: (Un)welcoming
Terri-Ceres de Roché-Puckerin: Vacant

BARNET
Taking the Tablets
RUTHIE RAPHAEL — WINNER

Ten weeks, three days, average for a stay on a psychiatric ward. They're ready to discharge me—the word conjures up an image of unclean underpants. I'm unsurprised; after all, I've been existing surrounded by thirty women in a confined space with just a cold shower. Is it any surprise I feel soiled? My ritual was to have an early morning shower, rushing out of bed as soon as the bathroom was unlocked, hoping to secure any hot water. The trickle of lukewarm water shocking against my goose-pimpled skin. I always loved the smell of a clean woman; no fragrance can compare. My mother smelled sweet like a fresh orange blossom. This bevy of women, in contrast, a mix of feral fear and overnight sweating, an olfactory dump heap.

Winter had set in during my hospital stay, the grey sleet and ice I was suddenly exposed to more welcoming than that hospital corridor.

Looking out of our dining room window into the garden, I watch the last of the winter leaves. The lawn carpeted with mushy brown remnants and rotten fruit of the once pregnant pear tree. A landscape, unattended by my gardener's hands. Abandoned, engulfed by a cold, dark habitual winter. It awaits the arrival of spring that will renew it to its colourful glory.

They called it a 'nervous breakdown'. I was assured that taking the tablets and time would heal my broken heart. I'm not ashamed, though many sufferers are. I am resilient, a fighter, I will find my whole self again. Depression—a fancy label to wear, in case the neighbours thought it may be something worse. Who wants a nutter living next door?

I eat my dinner at 8 PM, bucking the regimented regime of the 7 PM feed on the ward. After dinner I open a red velvet chocolate box, a gift from my chaplain. I'm amazed at the quality of these fancy chocolates, so unexpected a pastoral gift. At once I stake my claim. I have always been partial to nuts and almond praline. My husband stunned by the way in which I grab for and set aside those that 'are mine'. How can I explain what it is like to fight for food? The NHS is under-funded and the mental health system, her Cinderella. A chocolate, always a treat, now takes on a much deeper meaning.

Absorbing my old familiar yet somehow brand-new surroundings, the minutes tick by. I sit waiting—for what?

Sometime passes before I hear in my head an echoic voice that has now become a persistent reminder: 'Medication round, medication round!' Looking down at my watch it reads 10 PM exactly. Time I ought to be taking the tablets.

BARNET
Collateral Damage
SHEREEN PANDIT — HIGHLY COMMENDED

Two families of squatters moved in during that winter.

Possibly it was the unusually bitter weather that prompted the search for shelter. More probably it was that homes had been made available by the big fight Tara had with her mum just before the cold set in. The fight about Tara's failure to help with housework and gardening, to take responsibility for the home they all shared, blah, blah. It had ended with her slamming the shed door so hard that several of the panes shattered.

Tara's mum made her board up the gaps, but Tara obviously hadn't done a good job of the boarding up. That was how the two families got in. A garden shed isn't the most comfortable of lodgings, but the hedgehogs who settled in a corner of the shed floor had made a snug home. They'd helped themselves to bits from Tara's mum's ragbag, out of which they'd fashioned beds. Where the robins nested, Tara didn't find out until the end.

It was when she was glaring glumly out of her bedroom at yet another grey day, that Tara spotted some slight, slow movements barely visible against the grey brown of the lifeless garden. Hedgehogs. She felt her insides tingling with warmth as she watched the pair of hedgehogs, ambling across the garden, like two old people setting off for the shops.

Towards evening, closing her curtains, she saw them again, small shuffling shadows moving slowly towards the shed. They disappeared through a hole in the door and did not emerge again. Tara kept watch for them morning and evening. Sometimes she had to wait quite a while for them to emerge, probably off foraging for food, much like Tara's parents—well, just her mum now—going off to get groceries.

Tara's mum was thrilled about the hedgehogs. Apparently they were endangered and needed looking after. It wasn't a job Tara minded, putting out fruit and vegetables for them.

It was when she sneaked into the shed to do that, that she discovered the second family. She should have suspected from the noise and fluttering she'd seen when on hedgehog watch that birds had got into the shed as well.

Where in the shed the robins had nested, Tara couldn't see. Not until the spring that is, when her mum decided it was time to hang washing outdoors. Tara was in the midst of messaging with her best mate when her mum shouted for her to get the pegs.

She stomped to the shed. Forgetting about the hedgehogs and birds, she snatched the peg bag from its hook, spilling pegs onto the hedgehog bed. As Tara stuffed the pegs back into the bag, her hand touched some small smooth round objects. She peered into the bag. Robin's eggs nestled in a nest of twigs and some soft stuff. Hastily Tara rehung the bag, hoping the birds wouldn't notice she'd disturbed their nest.

The robins never returned. Nor did the hedgehogs. Nobody likes one's home messed with.

ENFIELD
House-Proud
PAMELA KANDEKORE — WINNER

Merle prepared a pot of cornmeal porridge for the family. After pouring herself a bowl, she ate whilst filling a pot of red peas for the day's soup. Then, for Sunday's dinner, seasoned chicken portions with chopped garlic, scallion, salt, black pepper and pimento, and picked out grit from a bowl of dried gungo peas before rinsing them. The toilet was already bleached from the night before, so by the time Merle mopped the kitchen and bathroom floors, the house smelled of food and bleach in equal measures.

It was dark in her front room and the aroma of lavender polish lingered from a previous clean. Merle squeezed past the furniture to reach the bay windows where she drew back a pair of heavy curtains. The daylight danced into the room, and even though dust particles jumped around and settled on her porcelain, she smiled at the net curtains she put up yesterday. No one window on Ashfield Road, or Hermitage Road, owned this set with its dandelion patterned trim. Yet, these curtains took a good portion of her pardner money, as well as energy. Merle struggled on the bus. Clifford couldn't drop her to Seven Sisters Road as he had to work a double shift.

There was laughter and the peep of a car horn outside. Merle surveyed Ashfield Road. It was not tree-lined like those on the other side of the borough, but each terrace had a front garden. At weekends, when the gates to the small factory were closed, children enjoyed cartwheeling, roller skating and riding chopper bikes across the road. Meanwhile, parents littered the pavement with home maintenance tools.

Alan, the next-door neighbour, cleaned his car and chatted to Kypros, who glossed his windowsills again. Sal painted his wall tiles red.

Last week, he painted his front door green and freshened the white walls. Merle at last stepped outside, frowning at the cracks in the floor tiles before her.

'Another change of curtains, Merle?' Sal called.

How him reach from his place, to be behind me gate? Merle puzzled. She kissed her teeth quietly before answering.

'I want my windows to gleam so I can watch everybody's business.'

'You should work for Selfridges—dress their windows!' Merle began to vigorously brush debris from the doorstep.

'Makes the rest of us look bad. Doesn't she Alan?'

Alan simply nodded and started trimming his privet hedge.

'It's all right for you lot,' Sal continued. 'I've got to paint *two* walls—being an end of terrace!'

Merle slowed her sweeping, thinking of a man who sold snow cones from his cart back home. He just about made a living from it. Because this Sal had an ice-cream van, he behaved like a rich man. When was the sun ever hot enough in England to eat ice cream anyway? Kypros owned the corner shop, Alan ran a taxi business, but Clifford earned a good wage on night shifts.

Lickle by Lickle, Merle. Don't put yu hat where yu han' can't reach.

ENFIELD
Africa My Ancestral Home
LISA HARDY — HIGHLY COMMENDED

The great continent of Africa, the home of mankind, the home of diamonds and gold, the home of iron and oil, the home of the first university in modern-day Mali, the home where my ancestors lived, the homes that were torn apart when people were stolen and brought of foreign shores, the traditions, languages and names that were left behind and forgotten, the people who did not get to return to their beloved homeland... until today that is.

As I take off my shoes to feel the heat from the red soil underneath my soft feet, the sandy dirt begins to sink in between my toes and its warmth travels through my bones and my blood as if it were recharging my battery. It instantly energises me, it brings me comfort and welcomes me home. The sun gently kisses each cheek like a grandmother would as it wraps itself around me with the warmest hug. The wind whispers in my ear like an old familiar voice I've heard many times before but cannot place. It says, 'Welcome home, my child, it's been a long time.'

This place, my ancestral home, makes my heart sing out loud in celebration. It makes me feel safe and secure, it makes me feel wanted and accepted, it gives me a sense of belonging and reuniting. It makes me want to throw both arms out and spin around in joy. My body wants to dance to the beat of the drums playing in my heart, I feel overwhelmed and thankful. I have returned home to my dearest Mother Africa, to walk on the same soil you walked on many years ago, to feel the very same sun that shone on your face many years ago, to have the same wind brush against my skin as it did yours many years ago.

I see a vision of beauty in the wild landscape, which is a symbol of freedom like my curly coily afro hair left to blow in the wind, the dark golden tones of my beautiful brown skin, like the mahogany that comes from the Khaya tree, my tall, slim, graceful frame stands proud like a Maasai warrior woman. Like many of the other tribes and those in the African diaspora we have developed an inner mental strength as well as an outer physical strength, we have battled through hundreds of years of oppression and maintained our courage to persevere, our endurance to survive and thrive in the bleakest conditions has now been forever ingrained in our DNA.

This is a new land for me but also an old land I have returned to. It's a new experience that somehow has a strangely familiar feeling. Traditional songs sing in my heart as the blood of my ancestors recognise those familiar beats. My body sways back and forth, my feet start to move up and down, my back arches, my chest opens as it rises and falls. I am home, mother dear, my dearest Mother Africa.

HARINGEY
(Un)welcoming
AISHA PHOENIX — WINNER

Tyra, Amerie's mum, paced up and down in the playground as she waited for 4C to come out. They were late, as usual, and she had to get back to cook for her colleagues. It was finally her turn to host them and making a good impression mattered—a lot.

'How you doing?' Kyle's mum said.

'Why are they always out late?' Tyra pulled at the baby hair at the back of her neck. 'I've got so much to do.'

Kyle's mum nodded as Tyra explained about the work dinner, all the dishes she'd promised to make and the drama that meant she was behind schedule.

'I could take Amerie home with me, so she doesn't get under your feet,' Kyle's mum said.

Tyra thought about how much time she would save if she didn't have to worry about her daughter. But then she knew Amerie and Kyle weren't exactly friends. Amerie had said he didn't particularly like her. 'So kind of you to offer, but it's OK. She has a life-threatening peanut allergy so, you know.'

'Don't be silly. She'll be fine. They can play Nintendo. And I'll just give them water and fruit.' Kyle's mum smiled.

The children began to join their parents. As Amerie bounded up, Tyra said, 'Kyle's mum has offered to look after you while I prepare for tonight.'

Amerie sucked in her breath and was about to speak, but her mum bent down and said in her quiet voice, 'It won't be for long and I'm really behind.'

As they walked away Kyle gave Amerie a look. Tyra almost called after them to say she'd changed her mind, but it was only for a little while and she would get so much done without having to entertain Amerie.

Tyra sliced her vegetables, then hacked her meat into manageable chunks. Her mind wasn't on her pumpkin soup or curry goat though, it was on the decision that stirred like indigestion in her stomach. Amerie would have happily peeled onions and crushed garlic or done anything else she'd asked. Should she really have sent her home with Kyle and his mum?

Tyra was browning the goat when the phone rang. She wouldn't have answered but it was the school.

'One of the pupils passed me a note after lunch that Kyle wrote. It was rather concerning,' Amerie's teacher said without the customary smile in her voice. 'We can discuss it more once I've had the chance to investigate, but it said: *If that girl Amerie ever comes to my house I'll kill her with a Snickers…*'

Tyra abandoned her cooking and ran down the road in her fluffy slippers. She arrived at Kyle's house, panting.

'Is everything OK?' Kyle's mum said.

'Where are the kids?'

'Upstairs. I haven't heard a peep out of them.' Kyle's mum smiled.

Tyra pushed past her and pounded up the stairs. On the landing she saw a brown chocolate wrapper with distinctive blue lettering and golden peanuts.

HARINGEY
Vacant
TERRI-CERES DE ROCHÉ-PUCKERIN —
HIGHLY COMMENDED

When she got home from work, he was dead.

She went to lift the body and then realised she couldn't touch it. He would be cold, stiff, unlike the quick and warm companion she had devoted the last three years to.

She wandered into the kitchen and washed her hands using mechanical thoroughness. She used a fresh dishtowel, rubbing all trace of liquid off her now-chapped skin.

Absently, she 'cooked' dinner: instant noodles on toast. A recipe she had discovered during her time at university and continued to eat nearly ten years later. She sprinkled some grated cheese and pieces of sliced ham on top, and then didn't eat. Watching it grow cold, the noodles and cheese congealed until the whole thing looked like creamy plastic. The plate sat neglected on the light wood countertop, an ornament of her inadequacy. Her stomach rolled.

She stumbled her way towards the bedroom. Here was darker than the rest of the flat, the large windows facing away from the setting sun. Welcoming the growing shadows, she fished her phone out of her trouser pocket. Scrolling through her recent messages, she tried to decide who to tell. There weren't a huge number of choices. She'd rather hurl herself into a thornbush than call Mother. Definitely not her bumbling line manager Darrel. Finally, she settled for Sharmane.

'Hello?'

'Heya, stranger! How are you?'

'Uh—Cosmo died.'

'*Who*?'

'Cosmo—you know, my—'

'Oh, yeah! Your hamster.'

'Gerbil.'

'Oh, OK. Listen, I've got to go—Henri-Kay's just got back from school in a strop. Chat later?'

Dull double beeps indicated the call had ended. Shocked, she stared at the now-silent phone. She raised her hand, ready to launch her phone across the room, and then with a defeated sigh dropped it lightly on the crumpled bed instead.

Armed with a dustpan and a cardboard box she had meant to recycle but never found the will, she went back to the living room. She carefully scooped Cosmo out of his tank and into the box which she then engulfed in tissue paper.

Having no access to a garden, she took the box of Cosmo outside and lumbered to the nearest park. It was chilly in a way that it hadn't been during the day and caught her by surprise. She shivered as she crouched by a thriving bush that smelled of heather.

'You all right, love?'

A large white man towered above her with his equally large white bulldog—who was suddenly sniffing intently at the Cosmo Box. She snatched it out of the bulldog's reach.

'Alfie, down. Oh—hi! It's Mike—from next door.'

She didn't know what to say except, 'My gerbil died. I was burying him.'

Mike's face softened. 'Sorry. I've got an allotment, if you'd like. We can do it there tomorrow. It's a hard thing, losing a pet.'

That was when she began to bawl loudly, unabashedly, in the middle of the park.

Mike helped her to her feet. 'C'mon, I'll walk you home.'

Central London

CAMDEN
Emily Gaywood-James: Lasagne for One
Tina Sang: The Way Home
S. Niroshini: Dearly Loved

CITY OF LONDON
Eleanor Sue Zhao: Hangzhou
Verity Greaves: Mausoleum

KENSINGTON AND CHELSEA
Alison Catchpole: Clearing
Stan Moorcroft: The Unspoken Pact

ISLINGTON
Hazel Beevers: Terra Incognita
Ashley Pegg: The Letter

LAMBETH
Tracey Hammett: Bare Earth
Khadija Badri: Fried Onions and Ringlets
Caleb Azumah Nelson: Closeness

SOUTHWARK
Emma Robertson: The Worry Bush
Jennifer McGowan: Housewarming
Lizzie Damilola Blackburn: Insta Story

WESTMINSTER
Loretta Ramkissoon: Home Safe

CAMDEN
Lasagne for One
EMILY GAYWOOD-JAMES — WINNER

I was eighty-three the first time I cooked for myself. Don't laugh. I know it's ridiculous. The truth is, Edie cooked all of my meals, unless we were going out to a restaurant or a dinner party or something. If she was unwell, or had gone out with friends, I'd usually just heat up a can of tomato soup.

I didn't need to know how to cook, I suppose that was my reasoning. It sounds so old-fashioned, doesn't it? Lola, my granddaughter, would say that I was profiting from the patriarchy, or something like that. She'd be right, of course, but it was just the way things were, in those days.

Edie was sharp as a knife, right up until she breathed her last. She remembered every recipe her mother had taught her, knew by heart the ingredients she would need for our daughter's favourite cakes. That was my undoing, really. She didn't need recipe books, so we didn't have any. When she died I didn't know where to begin. I would imagine her looking down at me standing in the kitchen, completely helpless, and I knew she'd be having a good laugh at my expense. Well, you're never too old to learn, that's what I told myself.

I started slowly. I took cookery books out of the local library, starting with those aimed at students, as I decided that, octogenarian widowers aside, they would probably be the most clueless in the kitchen. I told the librarian they were for my granddaughter, off to university, not that she asked. Anyway, Lola is a vegetarian, if you can believe it, and seems to live on something called tofu, so I'm sure she's much more advanced than I am in the culinary arts.

I left Edie's apron hanging from the hook on the back of the kitchen door. It made me feel like it wasn't quite real, like one morning

I'd be woken by the whistling of the kettle or the smell of bacon sizzling on the stove. Sometimes, I pictured her wearing it, standing at the counter making a trifle, telling me off for swiping amaretti biscuits before she'd had the chance to soak them in sherry. I bought a packet of the biscuits, but they didn't taste the same.

I was digging through the freezer a couple of weeks into my culinary journey when I found it. I was hoping to find a long-forgotten box of fish fingers that would excuse me from that evening's cooking, and I pulled out a Tupperware, labelled in her neat handwriting: lasagne for one. I gazed at the container, contemplating heating it up, but after a moment I slid it back into the drawer. While a meal she had made lay uneaten in our freezer, a part of her was still here, still home.

I stood up, knees creaking, and crossed the kitchen. From the top shelf of the cupboard, I pulled down a dusty can of Heinz.

CAMDEN
The Way Home
TINA SANG — HIGHLY COMMENDED

'Artwork is a map,' she once told me. 'Lines and curves contain cities of meaning, roads travel indefinitely on. It leads you where it desires to go.'

'It?' I asked.

'Your heart,' she said. She took my hand and placed it where the instrument thrummed and beat against my skin. 'What we perceive as art, the heart perceives as directions.'

She wove colour into paper, smeared thick lines of ink on intricate sketches, creating things nobody understood. In her last days, she fell into an artistic frenzy. Through the glass doors of her studio, I watched with wide eyes as she flung paint at her canvas, splattering walls and floor. She attacked her work with such intensity I figured there was something there I couldn't see; an invisible creature she stabbed at with her brushes, smothered with paint, gouged with intense, sharp strokes of charcoal.

'Something's gotten into your mother,' my father said at the dinner table when it was the two of us, which became often. 'She's going crazy.'

I silently watched her every evening, as she chased her invisible beast across the canvas. It left great blotchy footprints, and tracked lithe, snaking trails. And then one morning, I woke up to an eerie stillness that seized the house. Tip-toeing downstairs, I called out.

'Mom?'

Silence.

'Mom?'

My stomach churned. I stood barefoot on the cold wooden floor-boards a moment, before shouting for my dad. He came stumbling down, sleepy-eyed and dishevelled.

'Mom's gone.'

The calm in my voice made the air go still with finality. Grim phone calls and soft voices, dry faces painted with solemn lines. It was like we'd been preparing for her disappearance long before she left.

That night I lay in bed, heart pounding in the thick quiet. The stagnant air permeated my room, seeping into my lungs, choking me. Suffocated, I rose and went downstairs, nudged open the glass doors, and stepped inside. The moonlight drained the colours from the canvases, rows and rows of artwork dull and dead in midnight grey. On the easel rested her most recent painting; a steady black line marked her course across the canvas. Strong, purposeful, and continuous—until it petered out in the middle. Maybe the ink ran out, or the hand lifted from paper, or she simply decided to let go.

She left me directions in her manic sketches, insane scribbles, and broad charcoal lines. A final message, before she slipped through the seams of her canvas and raced away into the jagged, colour-stained realms of insanity. There's meaning encoded in the masterpieces. But I can't, for the life of me, understand what.

My finger runs along the length of the black road, tracing her marks. Tears carve routes down my cheeks, and my finger remains rested on the point where the line fades away.

I'll come find you, Mom. Just give me some time.

CAMDEN
Dearly Loved
S. NIROSHINI — EMERGING WRITER

A graveyard is a place of dreaming.

And in between the overgrown moss and lichen of Highgate Cemetery, the dead-folk of Swain's Lane spin dreams for the living each night. The work makes the air, here in the afterlife, sweet. It smells of lavender and freshly made lemonade. It is love-work, the warp and weft of memories turning into dreams as light reflects from the emerald-green foliage of the cemetery forest. It is impossible to hear anything over the din of chatter and laughter as the dead-folk work. It is through dreams the dead try and tell the living the single most important thing they need to know in life.

If only anyone listened.

It is a frosty February evening and I sit next to my headstone. I gather tufts of memory from my satchel to spin my granddaughter dreams. She arrives to the world of the living in eight days and I hope she listens to what the dead have to say. The dreams are as soft as marshmallow and fly through the air like the whip of a ship's sail. I have waited so long for this moment.

I remember the day I arrived at the cemetery. I don't know how I died but the first thing I noticed was how cool and damp it was, full of ivy. The second thing I felt was love.

In loving memory.
To my beloved.
Dearly loved.
It was a place of love.

My own headstone has a simple inscription. *Miss Anusha Alfonso, died 1872.* It says nothing of my life. How I had travelled the world, a young woman who had been one of the greatest playwrights to arrive in London. It doesn't of course include the smaller, intimate details; how I had many lovers, how I loved dandelions.

Only someone who truly cares about you will ever remember something like that.

The graveyard became a place where a woman like me could finally rest undisturbed. My mama used to say to me *you can sleep when you're dead* and oh don't I rest just perfectly now.

Ever notice how much sleep is like death?

Come. Help me spin dreams for my granddaughter. I need to move fast now. She has arrived early.

I'm not sure I'm ready for this moment but oh there she is asleep at the hospital on Pond Street. Healthy set of lungs on her. *Hush now, hush.* She is terrified of this transition to life from death. I wish she knew the great secret that the dead know, that life and death are the same. I lean down near her cot.

Everything is going to be fine, baby girl. We're always going home, always going into the arms of those who love us.

The dreams blow through her. Her eyes flutter as images of great beauty and love soothe her cries. She curls her little brown fist and falls asleep. Her breath is as soft as the fuzz of a dandelion.

CITY OF LONDON
Hangzhou
ELEANOR SUE ZHAO — WINNER

One of the certain joys of food is not in the eating but the preparation. My grandmother knew this most of all. Traipsing between stalls, the smell of vegetables during the hot summer—we'd go early in the morning to the market. Seven AM and bleary eyed, it was not joyous for my cousin, a few years older, who longed for the *good city life*. She was enamoured with an imagined existence, her angled symmetry, modern and deliberate.

For me the market was a peaceable novelty. There, my senses found a home. Market traders, not yelling like in London but sitting quietly, knowing that the business would come, not like goods traders; there was no bartering here. Still, my grandmother stood hunched at the okra stand, picking out the triangle-shaped vegetables attentively. And the seller, sitting pacific, was accustomed to her, or grandmothers like her. Life was simple, *certes*.

Curious, I would amble through the stands across the hall to the fish, poultry, live crabs and lobsters in giant tanks not giant enough to house tens, hundreds of living bodies; thrashing and drowning. Xing wei was always filling the air. In the afternoon, they would be subdued—oxygen a limiting factor. For now, they jostled against each other anxiously.

Is there such a thing as a good death? I wondered sometimes. *A better death, perhaps. A good enough death.*

You used to tell me that lobsters were intelligent, sentient. That was the summer you stopped eating octopus, and lobster, and pork, behoving me to do the same. But I loved takoyaki and my grandfather's hong shao rou; was too poor to eat lobster but wouldn't have resisted the opportunity. *There is a history to food*, I said, *a sacredness to protect.* You said, *History is meaningless when there is present suffering.*

It might have been inconsequential, absent the accusations and parables. As it was, like tectonic plates, we grated. A meat market, my grandmother's hunch, one hundred and fifty yuan for a delicious family lunch and a silence between us. Suddenly, there was a tension—of moral distinctions and distinct directions.

Life begets death. That was my reasoning. Not savage, cruel death, but dissipation. I always wanted to be buried, to give back. The thought of my body, degrading, feeding the earth was a comfort. *A return to form.* You dreaded the thought of being consumed by the ground. The realities mattered more, were ever more visceral and emotive than the philosophical. Like that, you saw the world with clarity and I loved you for it.

But someone once told me that there are two homes in life: the one you are born into and the one you make. Happiness is in the keeping of both, loneliness is in the keeping of none. Of course, I didn't understand but, playing along, I asked—*what is in the keeping of one?*

It depends, came the sagacious answer. *Joy, sometimes. And sometimes, grief.*

CITY OF LONDON
Mausoleum
VERITY GREAVES — HIGHLY COMMENDED

It was strange, the key turned easily enough. Alice thought there would be more resistance, the side door opened. She had to enter this way as there was no key to the front door. Alice glanced nervously round the kitchen, there was hardly an inch of floor space to walk on and the air smelled musty. She walked through the kitchen and into the hallway, what lay ahead seemed insurmountable to her, mountains and mountains of stuff, layers amongst layers of stuff. Stuff that held secrets, stuff that held stories, stuff to be sorted— made sense of—and stuff to be cleared.

The house had lain dormant and neglected for over ten years. It hadn't been habitable and had never been home to her. Alice had only been in this house once before, many years ago, and had come through the front door. More recently, she had cut the garden hedge but outside in the rain without a cup of tea or use of the bathroom. Alice remembered seeing the things piled high in the windows, not able to see in. When she'd left, she hadn't said anything, just imagined what lay behind the door of the house. It had been too difficult to confront and deal with, but now she had finally entered and could finally see her mother's possessions laid bare, a life lived, a life overcome by the things in it. This felt like an infinite task, her own personal Everest and this was only the beginning.

Alice was practically minded and organised, something she had learnt from a life lived in direct contrast to the woman she had just lost. She climbed up and onto a mountain of post in the downstairs hallway, it felt surprisingly stable. As Alice looked up, she could see a pathway up the stairs. She went to investigate the upstairs rooms, the bathroom had a bath storing a tower of old papers in it, there were two rooms you could hardly get into and her mother's bedroom which was the slightly larger and clearer room. This, she felt, would be the best place to start.

Alice got down to the task of sorting through the stuff and used the bed as a place to store and organise the things. She was curious as to what she would find, her mother had been a mystery and maybe in sorting the house, she would get to know who her mother had been.

The house was still, it was hard to be here only a day after her mother's funeral but the task of sorting, of uncovering and clearing would keep her busy. Earlier in the day, it had been gloomy and grey but suddenly in the late autumnal afternoon sun, a wonderful ray of light and warmth came through. Luckily, Alice found the key to the window which opened, and the fresh air and elements blew in. Alice felt something change, the outside had been let in and the house breathed into life.

KENSINGTON AND CHELSEA
Clearing
ALISON CATCHPOLE — WINNER

Endings always did
Have a habit of looking
Like new beginnings.

(I am not, thanks, lost,
Thanks, though at least not in the
Way you might expect.)

Home, after all, is
Wherever home can be—but
If no longer home

Then what?

Is home still home if
Those who made it sing, dance,
Home for us, are gone?

If the laughter and
The voices have faded, should
Home be somewhere else?

The need to clear when
The previous occupants are
No longer, well, in need,

Is a practical
Solution to the problem
Of the alchemy

Of death. And so when
The need arises, we clear
Necessary space.

Seeking solace in
An abandoned property
Seems both safe and strange.

And so begins a
Difficult but necessary
Process. Clearing. Space.

But it isn't just
About the endless boxes.
Homes hold so much more.

When I call upon
The love of life that once
Was so vibrant here,

That love which now seems
A glinting, melting liquid
Slipping through my hands

As I listen for
The cool, still sea that still hides
In that sea shell there

As I listen for
Sea and love and sunshine
And the air in between,

Can it be just that
I am no longer listening
Carefully enough?

Can the joy live in
The ornamental vases?
The folded clothing?

If I peer into
A dark cupboard of matter
Will the joy be there?

Could it be that if
The search continues, something
Once lost may be found?

Sounds, smells, thoughts chiming
To resonate and discharge
Their secrets and gifts.

They don't much relent
But neither does the sense of home
That they create.

Who are we tenants
Who merely inhabit and guard
These homes for others?

The laughter steeped in
Ageless feelings that used to be
Just children themselves.

This is where our end
And our beginning seem to
Meet and coalesce.

Indefinable
Home just is, always, a place
To rest and find out

What else might be out
In the wider world. So as
You unpack that box

As you consider
What to keep and what to move
To another life,

Imagine which things
Might serve a greater purpose
And find a new home.

Though just before you
Leave, go on your way, sidle
Onward and upward

Do look back. Do glance
And cast a thought to how it
Felt before the change.

The story which lives
In every part of this home
Is still unfinished.

And I would ask if
This gentle moment you
Could listen with me?

KENSINGTON AND CHELSEA
The Unspoken Pact
STAN MOORCROFT — HIGHLY COMMENDED

Mr Patel and I had a pact, an unspoken agreement. Unspoken being the operative word here, he did not comment on my purchases, and I refrained from the small talk. The pact suited my purposes: as the energy required for my daily trip for supplies grew, it drained away from the energy needed for washing, cleaning teeth, and getting myself dressed. The pact ensured that Mr Patel *never saw* that I was unshaven and was wearing my pyjamas under the slightly soiled sweater and jogger bottoms. It freed us both from any embarrassment.

Other customers, with whom I avoided eye contact, may have noticed, but not, it seemed, Mr Patel. The transactions always short, I placed two bottles of extra strong cider, or gin, or Special Brew, on the counter, sometimes preceded by a 'hi'. Money would change hands and to my relief the business was concluded.

Out of hospital for over a week, I have showered and dressed ready for the day, but I need milk. I have avoided Mr Patel and the corner shop since my discharge but hope the pact still holds.

I place the milk on the counter.

'You are not drinking?'

I am stunned, 'No, I am not drinking.'

'Good, I am pleased.'

'Thank you,' I take my change and return his smile. The pact is broken.

ISLINGTON
Terra Incognita
HAZEL BEEVERS — WINNER

All of us here know when someone new has arrived. When they turn up we each stand on our balconies to watch, some higher than others, but always looking down. Our block is on the busiest street in the busiest city in a busy world. Which means we see everything. We see those kids on the corner who play violins for people's change then go back up to the houses with four stories and front gardens. We see the dirty roofs of the 281, 91 and 17 glide past. We see shiny black cars pull up a little way in front—not too far but not too close—and a blonde gets in and out again in minutes.

It doesn't matter so much when the newbie arrives, but how. Joe was the first—third floor—drove his black cab right out front and parked it there ever since. It's a no-parking property which tells you everything you need to know about Joe. His wife and three kids just about squeeze in the lift with us all together and we all smile and look sideways when it judders upwards. The oldest teenager always nods to the beat in his headphones. After Joe was Ferhad; he turned up on his bike with just a bag. None of us have seen inside his place. Once we asked him whether he thought everyone in the world saw the same night sky and he snorted then said what does it matter, we're all here now. Next to Ferhad is Alina, she's a dentist with an elderly husband, two girls and a third on the way. Her place always smells of paprika and lemon cleaning fluid. And then there's Q, who got here on the 281 with his cat, says the new vets around here don't understand Clare's quirks and keeps her inside mostly.

One early morning when Alina's kids were just rubbing their eyes awake we heard the doors slam. We were expecting it. Joe turned his cab round to block the van and his son lay in front of it.

43

We went down and held Ferhad's soft, lined hand, saw his place for the first time; yellowing walls and a patterned rug. Don't worry, you're with us, we said. We heard the knocks on his door, made by clenched fists. We waited and listened, listened and waited. We patted white-knuckled fingers and smiled at each other, as Alina poured steaming tea from a pot.

We let that day yawn over us and pass us by. But probably none of us will forget it either, not because of what happened, but because it had become dusk and we were watching the starlings gather in a pink sky, moving towards each other and then away, rising and then falling, joining one by one so that they moved in a fluid wave of energy. Never quite together, but never quite alone.

ISLINGTON
The Letter
ASHLEY PEGG — HIGHLY COMMENDED

Katie opened the doors to the community centre. Trish was on the phone as usual.

'No, my bingo pouch, yes, on the windowsill, bring it with you. Yes, I've got to go.' She turned to Katie. 'Sorry, love, my husband, daft, you're in room five.'

Katie looked in through the nursery doors as she passed and glimpsed her daughter. She was a right chatterbox, not like herself. Katie hurried on to room five.

'Hi Katie, how are you?' said Carol, wearing a proper jacket and skirt as usual.

'I'm OK, thanks,' said Katie. She took out the letter and placed it square with her pencil case.

Carol cleaned the whiteboard. 'It's warm, isn't it?'

Katie was all right herself. 'Yeah.'

'Can you open the window?'

Katie got underneath it and pushed hard. Hot air from the crisped playing fields piled in.

A football slammed against the top window and Katie jumped back. The boy who'd kicked the ball was always pissing everyone off.

'Fuck off to school,' she shouted.

'You fuck off, fucking junkie,' said the boy.

'I don't do that no more!' Katie slammed shut the window and opened the local newspaper. Wanker!

'Maybe it is better closed. You didn't have to buy a newspaper. There are free ones,' said Carol.

'I wanted to,' said Katie.

'Did you find a headline you liked?' said Carol.

'Yeah, this one: Pen-sion-er pro-tests tree feeling, felling? I don't know what 'felling' is?'

'It's when you chop down something like a tree,' said Carol. 'Could you understand the article, the story?'

'The tree was planted when she first come on the estate. The council says it's too big,' said Katie.

'Good one, Katie. But we better wait. Mel's running late.'

'Usual story.' Katie handed Carol the unopened letter; she could only ask her. 'Can you help me with this? You can open it.'

'It's from Probation Service Victim Support. Darren's your ex-boyfriend?'

His name froze Katie's stomach.

'The letter's two weeks old?' said Carol.

She didn't know why she had delayed—it was better not to know. 'You was on holiday. I didn't want to ask anyone else,' said Katie.

'It says he is being released from prison early. He will be out on 11 July. If you need victim support you can call a number. Katie, that's today.'

Katie put her pens away. 'He'll go to my flat. I don't want him there,' said Katie.

She knew that Carol knew. Everyone bloody knew. When he punched her and left her unconscious, it was Trish who saw her through the window, while holding Emma's hand.

'He hurt you, didn't he?'

She felt embarrassed. 'Yeah.'

'He'll have some kind of restriction, like a restraining order or something, or a tag, surely?'

'He'll come, I know he will.'

'I'm going with you,' said Carol. 'Trish can find someone to look after Emma,' said Carol.

'It's not your business. You don't know him.'

'I won't let you do this on your own,' said Carol.

LAMBETH
Bare Earth
TRACEY HAMMETT — WINNER

'Who's responsible for the front garden?' Liz asked, after a couple of weeks of lockdown.

It was early spring, you couldn't travel far. People were going stir-crazy.

'Dunno.'

Jake wasn't bothered about the garden.

Liz hadn't lived with Jake long but she'd already grown accustomed to his indoorness. He wasn't one to take a walk. He mostly drove, and not far at that.

'It's such a mess, be good to plant something. People are desperate for a bit of outdoor space.'

The guy in the basement didn't care about the garden and the couple upstairs were cool, they even offered to pay for seeds.

Liz cut back the tangle of nettles and brambles, tugged at roots, cleared the crisp packets, glass bottles, woodchip fag ends and fox shit, found the skull of a small animal; she scattered packets of seeds and raked the soil over them tenderly.

Nature did its job. Soon small nubs nosed out of the earth, tiny green inhabitants, more and more of them, stretching upwards, reaching outwards, weaving and winding, budding and bursting, so that by June the whole space buzzed and hummed. Tender poppies nodded to blousy marigolds, bright blue cornflowers attracted the winks of the ox-eye daisies. There were flowers Liz couldn't even name, all amongst a riot of stems and leaves.

The weather warmed. People sat out on their steps. Passers-by stopped and looked and complimented the garden. The couple upstairs thanked Liz. The guy in the basement smiled.

Then temperatures rocketed. Amazon ran out of fans. People drank beer and got noisy and short tempered.

One night the people upstairs cranked things up, the bass so loud it made your chest vibrate. Windowpanes rattled in their frames. There was a scraping sound too, like someone had been gagged and tied to a chair and was dragging it along the floor to try to escape. It went on for hours. Jake couldn't understand how Liz could sleep through it. Sleep was impossible, he was on high alert, checking the clock.

By morning there was silence but Jake wanted revenge.

He built a tower of furniture with his Marshall speaker on top. It reached to the ceiling. He had to use an extension lead but he got it working OK… fixed it up to the music system, volume as high as it would go.

'Come on,' he told Liz. 'We're off out.'

He was white hot, seething and silent as he closed the door behind them and strolled away from the quaking house.

Liz could not relish their rare visit to the park, or the egg and chips they ate out to help out. All she could taste was the vinegar.

Hours later, when they returned, the house was still belching out distortion. But there was a strange stillness too. Jake strode up to the front door. 'Now we're even.' He turned to Liz but she wasn't there. She was standing in the middle of the garden and all around her was bare earth.

LAMBETH
Fried Onions and Ringlets
KHADIJA BADRI — HIGHLY COMMENDED

The smell of frying onions poured into the Tube carriage before it had stopped at the platform. It snaked from the hot dog stand at the Tube station entrance, down Khadija's nostrils and into the pit of her stomach.

Coming into Brixton was like tuning each sense into high definition. The assault of cold air rushing through the opening Tube carriage doors triggered an involuntary intake of breath, and a buckling of the shoulders to protect exposed earlobes.

Out on the street, incense dispersed overlapping notes of sandalwood, jasmine, cinnamon and lemongrass over the wall of bodies advancing in every direction; towards the O2 Academy gig, the Tube station, the bus stops scattered up and down Brixton Road, the eateries representing almost every continent nestled in Brixton Village. The shouts of the preacher punctuated the crowd, calling on passers-by to find Jesus.

Khadija weaved through the throngs of people, her eyes searching for the numbers 432, 415 and 2 on the faces of approaching buses. Before moving to Tulse Hill, she had never given much thought to the expression 'you wait ages for one bus and three come along at once'. Yet all three of her buses always seemed to be attached to one another.

Sitting on the bottom deck of the 415, conversations in Spanish and Portuguese interlaced with phone calls in patois drifted around Khadija. Her eyes rested on the springy, black coils of hair magnificently framing the woman's head in front of her.

Khadija looked at her reflection in the window; framed by a looser set of dark curls, betraying her Arab roots. Curls she had only learned how to nourish upon moving to London, where shops for curly and textured hair were within walking distance. Where she could find a butcher's selling merguez sausages. Where people didn't ask whether she was mixed race, or what exact mix of races she was.

Khadija thought of the conversation where Mum had asked whether she had always known she wanted to move to London. Khadija hadn't, nor could she have predicted how comfortable she would feel existing in her own skin once she did.

When her best friend Emma had visited for the weekend, as they walked into King's Cross station to say goodbye, Emma had said, 'I get it now.'

'What do you mean?'

'I always thought jobs must have been the reason you were willing to pay ridiculous rent for houseshares while we were all putting down deposits. But when I first got on the Tube, I saw a girl that reminded me so much of you. She was wearing her curls on top of her head like you always do.'

Her adopted home city could often feel like the loneliest place in the world, surrounded by strangers, each with busy and important lives of their own, and so far away from her lifelong friends scattered across various northern cities.

And yet, Khadija stayed.

She stayed, and she belonged.

LAMBETH
Closeness
CALEB AZUMAH NELSON — LEAD WRITER

All of us at the party are already nostalgic for yesterday, so it's grime cuts that Adeline spins from the decks. '21 Seconds', 'I Spy', 'Too Many Man'. 'Pow' begins to play, a kick drum starting off, sudden and sure. A thick bassline follows, getting to the heart of things. Eerie chords ring round the garden. Before the intro is done, Raymond magics himself next to me, calling for the song to start again. There isn't time for what I want to say to him before the song starts fresh, the intro bare and empty of words, leaving space for us. The floor clears, bare and empty of bodies, a circle forming around us, something possessing Raymond and I as we push the edges further towards the confines of the garden. Look, I'm trying to tell you what it means to be in the eye of a mosh pit: a small, beautiful world in the midst of chaos, free, amongst, flailing limbs and half-shouted lyrics. Soon, after the fifth or sixth reload, we begin to tire. Soon, we're disappearing into the night, four abreast down Walworth Road, in search of food. Soon, it's Bagel King, the only place we know that's open forever. Soon, it's Raymond with an arm around my shoulder, mouth to my ear, saying, *you good, yeah,* and I nod into the space he makes. Soon, it's an arm wrapping around my body from behind, and I know it's Del. We've known each other so long she knows the way light holds my neck, she knows my rhythm, even when I'm still. Soon, it's a cappellas and phone speakers, and since the one thing which might solve most our problems is dancing, an easy two-step on the pavement.

Soon, too soon, it's time to split. Those who are together disappear into the night, pulling even closer. Those single long for the knock of knees on a journey home, the brush of skin on the doorstep, the invitation inside a free yard. We're young and often struggle to express just what it is we need, but I know we all value *closeness*.

That's what I'm thinking as Del and I take the night bus back towards Peckham—Raymond has magicked himself elsewhere, into the night, so it's just me and her. Her soft cheek resting on my shoulder for the short journey. Off the bus, arm in arm, down her road, a soft light on her doorstep, like a beacon. It's just us. It's the quietest it has been all evening. I gaze at her. Thrust my hands into my pockets, breaking the gaze with a glance at the ground, before stealing another look at her. She smiles at my shyness, and I smile back. It's here, when I'm with her, I know that a community can be two people, occupying a space where we don't have to explain. Where we can feel beautiful. Where we might feel free.

Del's lips make a brief home on my cheek, and we pull each other close. We give no goodbyes—we know death in its multitudes, and goodbye sounds like an end—instead, after our embrace, the soft pounding of fists accompanied by, *in a bit*, which is less a goodbye, more a promise to stay alive.

SOUTHWARK
The Worry Bush
EMMA ROBERTSON — WINNER

'Here.'

The girl pointed to a bush, indistinguishable to me from the other surrounding greenery, as if unveiling a fine work of art. I glanced at my big brother for guidance but Pete was frowning, as if he couldn't find the words; still, I liked this girl with the puffball skirt and shiny patent shoes with a bow on them and I wanted to please her, so I pulled my face into an approximation of wonder and delight. 'Wow!'

'It's the best thing about this house,' she enthused, patting a leaf lovingly as Pete and I shrugged at each other. 'If your parents move here, you can come and tell it all your worries.'

'Why?' Pete was smiling now.

'It listens. It does,' she added, turning to me as Pete walked away laughing. 'I'm serious.'

Five months later when the paperwork was complete and our parents had installed the new avocado bathroom suite and torn out the original wood-burning stove and fireplace to replace them with the modern electric appliances that my mother craved, I ventured down to the garden to take another look at the bush.

'Hi, Worry Bush,' I whispered, looking around to check that Pete wasn't nearby. 'I'm worried about starting my new school on Monday.'

I waited, then it occurred to me I didn't know what I was waiting for. The girl had never said that the bush answered, had she? Feeling foolish, I turned to walk away when a light breeze caused the leaves to rustle. I hesitated; was it my imagination or did the bush just tell me that things would be fine? I looked closer at the sturdy, olive-green leaves and at once believed that there was wisdom held in its proud form. You'll make new friends, it seemed to say. Don't worry.

From then on, I told it all my fears and problems. It listened when I fell out with my new friends and sympathised when I wasn't allowed to see Haircut 100 in concert. I was angry with it for a while when my Gran died. 'You said she wouldn't die!' I sobbed into its leaves.

No, came the reply on the breath of the wind. I said not to worry about her dying. She was in no pain and her life was complete. Don't be sad.

My greatest fear was for our family when Pete moved out. 'He's moved to London to live with his friend Jack and my parents say we aren't going to visit him. They're always so angry now.'

Give them time, I heard through the swoosh of the leaves. They're trying.

I'd almost given up hope, but at Christmas Pete brought Jack home and everyone stood around stiffly, silently. Eventually, Dad shook Jack's hand and offered him a glass of home brew, and even though Jack glanced longingly at Mum's glass of Mateus rosé, he accepted. I saw Pete smile for the first time in ages and outside, the frost-tipped Worry Bush twinkled in the breeze.

SOUTHWARK
Housewarming
JENNIFER MCGOWAN — HIGHLY COMMENDED

I am holding myself like a thin-stemmed wine glass, monitoring the second hand on the kitchen clock. When your name pops up on the screen, I shatter.

The call connects and the first thing I see is your screen reflected in the lenses of your glasses. A miniature thumbprint of me, looking at you, looking back at me. They are the thick-rimmed glasses you bought in the early 90s—the ones you are wearing in the photo of us at Christmas that sits on my desk. You wear your smile like a light linen jacket. Your gentle breeze drifts through the laptop and smoothes the creases of my forehead.

You look like you've been sleeping but when I ask you if you've just got up, you turn the question round on me.

'I've been very productive, thank you very much!' I laugh, gesturing to my overalls and the freshly painted yellow of the kitchen wall.

'Are you gonna give me the tour then?'

I carry you around the house. You laugh when I show you the photo of me in my slippers pointing at the sold sign. You tell me not to worry that the orchids haven't bloomed in a little while and that they need to rest through winter. When I point to the record player, I can't tell whether the screen has frozen. But when I ask if you remember it, you nod your head. You remember, too, that I stopped listening to music when you died.

I take you outside and point out the pair of parakeets on my neighbour's roof. I pick up a cup of coffee from Nunhead Lane and we wander instinctively up to the cemetery. You tell me not to get a dog, knowing that I'm going to do it anyway. You seem pleased that I'm still writing. And that I'm still in touch with the people you know from home.

You don't ask about the man I'm going to marry and I don't blame you. Instead you want to know what the air smells like here and what I'm planning to grow in my garden. I show you the place near the cemetery where we picked blackberries last September and you close your eyes as I describe the crumble we baked. The sweet fog that rose from the oven and the blood-red berries that stained our chins.

When we get back home, you look tired, as if you've done the walking too, so I take you to the couch and light the fire.

The flames slow-dance in your lenses, fatigued by the distance they have had to travel.

'I'm just resting my eyes,' you say. And I keep the laptop open so I can still hear you breathing.

SOUTHWARK
Insta Story
LIZZIE DAMILOLA BLACKBURN — EMERGING WRITER

Phone in hand, she enters Boots and strolls towards the makeup section. She passes rows of identical-looking bright display stands: neat lines of lipstick in red and pink hues; ice-cube-looking trays boasting pastel-coloured, neon and metallic eyeshadow; round palettes of cream foundation sporting ivory, beige and the occasional brown, smudged with grubby fingerprints.

She stops at the stand with the most variation of mocha, scans the lipsticks and picks up two reds: flamenco and cherry. She hovers her phone over her palm, takes a picture and uploads it to her Insta Story with the caption, 'Hmm. Which one should I go for?' She goes for the cherry.

Next stop, M&S. She makes a beeline for the wine aisle, grabs a bottle of Pinot Grigio. After a number of U-turns, she locates the plastic flutes and heads to the self-checkout tills. She's about to stuff the items into the 10p plastic bag, when she fishes out her phone, takes a photo and uploads it to her Insta Story. 'Someone's getting spoilt today,' she types, followed by a winking face emoji.

All the way to the car park, her phone buzzes in her coat pocket. Just before she drives off, she checks her Instagram: thirteen reactions, mostly from people she doesn't know.

'Enjoy your date!' Xina_1990 says, followed with a smiley face.

She stashes her phone away and makes the thirty-minute drive.

Despite knowing the way, the nurse leads her to the room; the familiar smells of lukewarm rice pudding lingering in the corridors. She smiles, perches on the chair beside the bed and places a hand over the frail, veiny one which once held her to her bosoms and nursed her.

'Happy birthday, Ma.' Her voice cracks. Meanwhile, her mother, through milky, blood-flecked eyes stares at her with a familiar look of bewilderment. Truthfully, she too, barely recognises her mum, what with her winter-white hair and gaunt cheeks dappled with brown skin tags and liver spots. The woman who was once upon a time the life and soul of every party. But she promised herself that she would continue to celebrate her mother's birthday the way she used to, the way she would have.

'I brought you some of your favourite things,' she says, placing the recently purchased items on a nearby table.

Her mother just blinks at her.

She places a hand over hers again.

After a few minutes, her mother's eyelids become too heavy and flutter close. Gingerly, she slithers her hand away and reaches for the lipstick and, as light as a feather duster, she dabs it on her mother's cracked lips. After, she tops a flute with wine, and while holding it by the spine, she rests her head against her mother's. Awkwardly, she raises her phone and takes a few photos.

She stares at one; tears prick her eyes.

Blowing out her cheek, she taps on Instagram, gloop bubbling in her stomach like acid. She closes it.

Some moments are just meant for you.

WESTMINSTER
Home Safe
LORETTA RAMKISSOON — WINNER

The perfume she'd sprayed on her hair from the tester bottle in Selfridges blooms roses as you release her from your tight embrace outside the restaurant. It had been too long.

'It was so good to see you.'

'We need to do this more often.'

'Definitely. Text me when you get home.'

You go one way; she goes the other.

As you walk, the energy from the Pinot Grigio, pasta and joyful conversation fills you with warmth, despite the noticeable drop in temperature. You take the Tube, a slow shuddering journey, and when you exit the sky is the colour of fountain-pen ink. You wrap your scarf around your neck. You choose the route with the most traffic, the most people, the most light, the most chance. No earphones. You make sure no one is close enough to steal your phone before you take it out to check for messages, then shove it back down into your coat pocket. You fish for your keys in your handbag and let them rest in the cold creases of the gaps between your fingers.

Your footsteps echo as you reach your front door and the key finds the keyhole without hesitation. You shut the outside world out. You made it. The flat is dark; still. You put the kettle on and send a message.

Home now. Are you back OK?

You put your phone to charge, sip your tea and wait for the screen to light up with a reply.

*

You lie in bed restless. The pillow already too warm. She said she was meeting a friend for an Italian in Soho. You imagine the saline juice oozing out of the mussels, the plumpness of the prawns, the light heat of chilli on the seafood linguine she always orders, followed by the richness of a cloying chocolate mousse. It's only 10 PM. Still early. But you won't sleep. Not until you hear the click of the key in the lock, the creak of the front door opening, shoes being kicked off in the hallway, the flush of the toilet.

The years of preparation for the bad that slices through the good in this world started early. You think about the times you told her to never accept sweets from strangers, never let go of your hand, never get into a car — even if they seem nice. You tell her to make sure the taxi she books is registered, to text her friends her location and to always, always call if she needs anything. Because you wouldn't think twice about getting out of bed in your tired pyjamas and going to her. Every time she leaves the house, you hope that the good will prevail.

*

The shadows from the trees keep you both company with whispers until it happens.

Sleep will not come because you are waiting for the buzz, the ping, the click, the flush, the sounds of human life. The sounds that mean home safe.

East London

BARKING AND DAGENHAM
Shahema Tafader: Hasten to Prayer
Donna Thomson: Plum Jam

BEXLEY
Toyah Panton: Anchor of Hope
Robert Butler: The View from Mars

GREENWICH
S M Smith: Broken Wings
Maureen Stapleton: Move or Stay?

HACKNEY
Erin Niimi Longhurst: The Kettle
Noah Birksted-Breen: Ten Steps from Home
Jarred McGinnis: We Sleep in These Sheets

HAVERING
Shupaula Mistry: That Heart-Break Thing
Amanda Wynne: Home Improvements

LEWISHAM
Ruth Bradshaw: The Gathering
Harry Irvine: The Alternative Case Note: 'Aluna Moved to a New Foster Placement'

NEWHAM
Jay A Gee: A Prison Gets to Be a Friend
Marjorie Browne: The Nice One

REDBRIDGE
Anneliese Amoah: Waiting for God
Jenny Gibson: Like the Turtle

TOWER HAMLETS
Rosaleen Lynch: Gummy Bears
Tom O'Brien: Maginy
Natasha Brown: The Alderton Farm: Interview with Claire Spencer

WALTHAM FOREST
Sam Burt: Accommodating
Christina Carè: After
Iqbal Hussain: All Her Tomorrows
Ruth Goldsmith: ▮▮▮

Hasten to Prayer
SHAHEMA TAFADER — WINNER

Malaikah stared at Daddy's undies with a smile, her fingers stroking her chin as though Santa's beard sprouted there. The green pants were placed on the floor beside the table holding the telly.

Daddy was getting the mats out behind her. A small one for him to stand on while leading the prayer, and a long one made for five people.

Malaikah turned to see Daddy putting a white hat on his balding head—a tokki. He readjusted the long skirt around his waist and a memory rushed in.

'You monkey, it's not a skirt. It's a lungi.'

'But it looks like a skirt, Daddy.'

Daddy laughed and said, 'Yes, well, it's what us Bengali men wear for comfort.'

'Yes, Daddy, skirts are comfortable.'

To her left, Mo, her eight-year-old brother, came into the sitting room. She smiled, rushed to him, pulled him down and whispered in his ear.

Mo placed his hands on his back and straightened himself, as though plagued with arthritis. He raised his fingers to his chin, looked up for a few seconds, then nodded.

Together, they ran to the bedroom and rummaged through Daddy's drawer, like mice foraging for morsels. Malaikah found a blue-and-white striped lungi, and Mo found a green one. Mo took off his trousers then helped his sister take hers off. He put both lungis on the floor and pushed them around till they made circles the small bodies could step into. Inside their respective rings they pulled up the lungis and tied them around their chests.

Even then the lungis trailed the ground like wedding gowns.

Malaikah followed her brother as he lifted his lungi and ran back to the sitting room, to the green undies. Here, each took off their knickers and pants and placed them next to their father's. A yellow one and a blue one, barely a third of the size of the green one.

Their father was already standing on the small prayer mat, facing away from them. He cleared his throat and called: 'Allahu akbar, Allahu akbar.'

God is the greatest. God is the greatest.

Mo grabbed his lungi at the front, like the ugly sisters in Cinderella, and trotted to the mat behind his father.

Malaikah tripped and fell.

'Ashhadu an la ilaha illa Allah.'

I bear witness there is no god except Allah.

Malaikah pushed up to her hands and knees, twisted to sit down, then pulled at the lungi till it uncovered her feet.

'Hayya 'ala-s-Salah. Hayya 'ala-l-Falah.'

Hasten to prayer. Hasten to success.

Malaikah held the lungi above her knees and scurried beside her brother.

'Allahu akbar.'

Mummy put a scarf on Malaikah's head and joined them on the mat behind daddy.

'La ilaha illa Allah.'

As Daddy recited the prayers, Malaikah felt a breeze like the summer air and a lightness like floating through clouds. She could see why her daddy liked wearing a skirt over his bare bottom.

BARKING AND DAGENHAM
Plum Jam
DONNA THOMSON — HIGHLY COMMENDED

Home was a whisper, a dream that you had awoken from many times.

Childhood memories of picking wild berries, blackberries and raspberry thimbles on fingertips, chasing and running and applying huge dock leaves to legs stung by stinging nettles.

The delightful stomping on mounds of berries, squealing as the juice squirted onto bare legs and chubby arms.

Large pots on the stove stewing the fruit, adding sugar, decanting once cooled into jars and vats that covered every spare surface in the kitchen. My aunt Celia stirring happily, and my grandmother, how sickly sweet the smile was on her face as she sat in her chair, dementia-ridden and glassy-eyed watching the bustle in the kitchen but not really taking it in, for she too had become a whisper.

One such memory that may have happened many times was ruckus in the kitchen, awakening hazily and descending the stairs and being met with glass in the kitchen, an uncle in a stupor and jam on the floor, more often than not plum, the fruit of which still made me wince on sight, for plum was our most favourite of all the jams my aunt made. I always checked on my grandmother on my way back to bed and there she was, in bed, glass-eyed, in bed, a strange little smile on her face, I pulled her bed throw up around her and she paid me no heed as I kissed her forehead.

It wasn't until the night my aunt had called me many years later babbling of blackberries and Victoria plums and of Uncle Wendel's supper that I packed my carpetbag and made haste back to the street lined with trees and fields of blackberries in the back and wildflowers in the yard to the little house with the yellow door in which I had once lived.

'Oh Lily, Lily,' said my aunt as I trod upon the musty carpet, the air was damp and the windows heavy with condensation.

'Have a biscuit,' said my aunt, directing my glance to the saucer on my uncle's side table, fondant cream sandwiched biscuit of different varieties.

'Hello, Uncle.' I leaned over him to get a biscuit, it didn't surprise me in the slightest that he was still in that very same chair as he had been when I left. He stared at me, eyes pools of black, and I bit into the biscuit, it was soggy and had lain there much too long I fancied.

'Tea, Lily. Come let us go and make some tea', my aunt enthused, and I of course obeyed.

'I don't imagine you want tea, Uncle, do you?' I asked, and as expected, no response. I patted his shoulder and left him where he was, still propped up dead in his wingback chair, and followed my aunt to the kitchen.

BEXLEY
Anchor of Hope
TOYAH PANTON — WINNER

When I asked you what your name meant we were in the basement of a hidden bar in East London, with iridescent lights that reflected the richness of your dark skin. You positioned yourself closer, to formulate a whisper, as if to maintain secrecy of your name's meaning, as if it were sacred. Slowly and gently, you shared the words 'servant of the almighty'. Your whisper slowed time and I felt calmness as your heartbeat invaded my chest, as our bodies remained pressed together, colliding into one. I smiled in response to the magnitude of your name, and you reverted the question back to me. 'Fruits of God,' I said responding proudly. Your eyes lit up and at the same time shrank as you smiled your wild toothed smile which always communicated more than your words alone.

I clung to that memory of our first embrace as my bus journeyed its way through tight pockets that were the backroads of Lewisham. This was only date number two but already we knew—we had a certainty about each other that remained unspoken but simultaneously was out in the open. I arrived at your doorstep in Streatham around 8 PM, it was my first time visiting your house and you were keen to host as your place was new to you. Also new to you, was my beloved city—you who had moved from Texas two months ago, ventured here on a mission to expand the footprint of your architectural brand and chose South London for its potential to inspire young Black girls and boys to enter the industry. I admired you for being averse to risk—in ways you reminded me of everything I was not. Whilst you were well travelled, I had lived all my twenty-six years in London, not having seen much of the world beyond. My attachment to London could be explained by a few things—my admiration of the tall buildings with pointed noses, the epochs of culture and history existing in micro-communities, the vibrancy and busyness, where people and transport know nothing of stillness.

You welcomed me into your abode with a warm hug and took from my hands the bottle of Shiraz, which you poured into wine glasses that you had already laid aside. The darkness of the sky invaded your flat, the sounds of London sounded mean as police sirens and human voices rattled in competition for attention, but in your arms, I felt safest. It's as if this city was made for me and for you, with just us two nothing else mattered. As we sat in the darkness of your living room with our hearts content, our bellies full and our souls searching for the mysteries within each other, I realise that it is you who will teach me a new meaning of home, it is you who will show me something unsearchable in this city I know, it is you who will become my anchor of love and hope.

BEXLEY
The View from Mars
ROBERT BUTLER — HIGHLY COMMENDED

Ebba takes a last look around the half-empty habitation dome. There's the faded poster of blue Earth that her father put up so long ago. The scribbled drawings she made on a wall when a kid. Mum made her scrub at them but they stayed there, stubborn as cave paintings. The background sound of the air-cleaning unit, still making its *tick-tick-woosh* sound. Dad used to tell her a grumbling gremlin lived inside it.

Through the scratched porthole of the kitchen window is the familiar scene of Mars. Once it was orange-red, dusty and dry, but she's seen it change and now it is a fertile patchwork of tall, glaucous plants, intermingled with mosses and lichens, under a butterscotch sky.

Ebba's gaze flickers onto a shelf. Several seashells glow palely in its shadows. She walks over and picks up a pink-white spiralled conch, holding it to her ear. The susurrus of her blood whispers up a sea sound. The shells were from her first visit to Earth. Or maybe it was the second, unhappy trip. After Mum's accident. But what Ebba remembers is the shock of seeing the gigantic, unending ocean for the first time, the enormity of water, its profligate, uncaring profuseness. Seeing the waves rolling in towards her, the salty spray hanging in the air, moistening her skin, fingering her lips and hair.

Her flight allowance is almost full. The shells weigh little. She tucks them into her spacesuit pockets.

A corridor leads to the astro dome. Her brother has already claimed Dad's telescope. Her father had religiously tracked Earth, ready for when it swam into view.

'Well, I'd better be going then,' Ebba says out loud. *Tick-tick-woosh* says the room. Suddenly tearful, she picks up her bags and walks into the airlock chamber, its door sliding solidly into place behind her.

Twenty years earlier
Through the kitchen window I watch my daughter Ebba grubbing around in the red soil, pushing young plants into the crumbly matrix, her fingers stubby in her suit's gloves. Between her efforts and Mars's radiation, they have a tough challenge. But the genetic tweaking should give them a chance. She wipes a hand against her helmet, leaving its glass smeared red, the familiar blood-streak of us would-be Martian farmers.

There's a beeping on my comms system. Natasha is calling from somewhere high overhead, her space tug doing its dance amongst the cargo ships.

'Hi darling,' she says, through the static. She sounds so tired. 'I'm going to work some extra shifts, I'll be down in a couple of days. It'll help us out.' A pre-recorded message. I'll call her later when she's free.

Soon I will walk along to the telescope. Earth is visible. That waterworld shows me we are salt beings, carrying the ocean around with us, our evolutionary beginnings, no matter where we are or how far we venture. I suppose in a way our tears are a small, jewelled reminder of that.

GREENWICH
Broken Wings
S M SMITH — WINNER

Popping out the first, second, then third, she peers under her bushel to inspect the dispatch. All seem present and correct, but just to make sure they have viability, she nudges them with her beak. Two of her eggs resist the push and stay firm on their delivery bed, but the third rolls with wanton abandon. It is an empty promise, so she flicks it out of the nest and, on landing, the shell splinters with a rainbow of bloodied yolk snaking out.

Pushing the two remaining eggs together she delicately but firmly bears down, fanning and flapping out her feathers, cocooning herself around the birth bulbs, and patiently waits.

*

Happening upon her by chance, glimpsed on his horizon, he had spiralled high above to watch the majesty of her flight. A new love interest he had thought, preparing to arrest her attention. But he evidenced she was already taken, for in her beak she held fast a clutch of twigs; the cargo being posted into the belly of an oak tree.

With his puffed chest deflated, he now stalked her further comings and goings with a different kind of interest.

And waited patiently.

*

The wait is nearly over. The warm ambience has ripened the embryos into lifeform where, outgrowing their jellied cell, they start to scrape, scratch and peck at the walls. Finally, they pierce through. Writhing in their now-empty sacs, they make to stand on pin-thin legs, but their spindles will not support balloon bellies and so collapse, to embark on a pitiful chorus of squawking, heralding to him their birth.

*

Born hungry, from history, she knows their cries will fade to empty if food is not swiftly delivered. She shuffles to the edge of the nest, spreads her wings and, with one forceful flap, pitches herself skyward with the liquor of birth being whipped beneath her. She centrifuges, pressing her wings tight to her body to streamline her flight to soar high above the canopy of trees, then tailspins to pitch on the brown canvas.

*

Arriving simultaneously, he scratches with disinterest at the earth which itself offers hollow return. She however has purpose and intent, so plunges her beak deep to pluck a colony of thick pink worms where, with bundle secure, she propels herself homebound. He also takes flight.

*

On hearing snapping twigs, the new-borns jostle impatiently for position, their translucent beaks stretched to near splitting, gobbling air. He silences their thin cries by piercing his talon through the canopy of a wing to dispatch one, the other he mangles underfoot. He rolls the bodies through the nest to make a bloodied ball and delicately but firmly scoops the mass inside his beak. Clamping it shut to secure his load he launches himself skyward and homebound.

*

Both are pleased with their haul, for with feasts fat in mouths, one has the knowledge, the other the belief, their offspring will survive the coming days.

GREENWICH
Move or Stay?
MAUREEN STAPLETON — HIGHLY COMMENDED

Penny's pen was poised above the paper.

'What do you think?' she asked her husband, nodding in the direction of the redeveloped flats looming in front of them with their sandblasted brick, black-framed industrial windows and spare urban landscaping.

Charles considered the question while he tossed his house keys from hand to hand, the same set he'd used since 1964.

'Hard to say,' he finally replied. 'Maybe the answer will be clearer once we work our way through the question.' A retired university professor, Charles loved to discuss any problem ad nauseum to find a solution. He also hoped the more they talked, the less Penny would want to move.

'Fine,' she said, as her pen moved across the page, underlining 'Move or Stay?' at the top. Penny loved a list.

When they bought their Georgian house as newlyweds in the 1960s, it was an eye-watering amount of money for them, but now would be the cost of a used car. Back then, this part of London was as far from trendy as John O'Groats was from Land's End. 'South of the river?' some friends said at the time, their noses wrinkling at the thought.

Their daughters had been pestering them for months about going to visit the new flats. Using their parental intuition, which always surprises children no matter what their age, they knew their younger daughter had a secret agenda behind the entreaties. She wanted their house for her growing family and hoped she could strike a deal with her parents. Sentiment aside, it was in a good catchment area.

'We'd need to clear the house,' Charles said, thinking of the books, the knick-knacks and the general detritus that had accumulated after so many years. 'We might need a skip.'

Penny wrote 'House clearance' and 'Skip?' in the 'Stay' column.

'Won't you miss the garden?' Charles asked, thinking of their towering white rose bushes and the endless games of cricket with the girls, and now the grandchildren.

'I won't miss the weeding,' Penny said. 'I can put some flower pots on the balcony. We both know our house is entirely too big for us now. It's time to go somewhere new.'

Penny wrote 'Garden' and 'Too Big' in the 'Move' column.

'What about all the memories we have there?' Charles asked. 'We can't move the door with the pencil marks showing how the girls grew. We can't move the stair where you gave birth the second time. Lots of things happened there.'

'We can bring the memories with us. They don't even need boxes,' she said. 'We know the girls are all grown up. We don't have to walk past a marked-up door every day to remind us of that.'

'But it is nice to see,' he said. Back at the house, the ghosts of the past smiled.

'True,' she said, sighing. She wrote 'Memories' in the 'Stay' column.

Penny put her list away. They walked up the hill, hand in hand. To home.

HACKNEY
The Kettle
ERIN NIIMI LONGHURST — WINNER

Last night we had to call the locksmith. The backdoor had jammed, again, and for the past month we had taken to lifting the door, shifting its entire weight within the frame in order to allow for it to click into place and swing open.

The sudden frosty spell we'd been having had made the old door more stubborn and curmudgeonly than ever, and so we had to seek professional help. And help came, armed with his box of well-worn tools.

I offered him a cup of tea, as you do, and began to fill my kettle.

Its white enamel is chipped, it's scratched in places, and they definitely aren't in fashion, these whistling kettles, but having moved from place to place, country to country, home to home, it's been a comfortable and constant companion.

My partner hates the sound it makes—and judging by his reaction, the locksmith does, too. But I think it's wonderful.

I think it's clever, the way it harnesses chemistry and physics to let us know it's ready. It unapologetically lets you know it's time for tea, filling the kitchen with sound like an opera singer in a music hall. For that reason alone you'll never catch me with an electric one, which feels clinical and sterile for reasons I can't quite articulate in a way that would make sense to anybody else.

This kettle has served me like a compass, its constancy as I try different locales on for size removing a variable in my little experimental search for home.

As if trying to calibrate coordinates, I'd make cups of tea, the flavours changing and adapting depending on my location. If the water was too soft, the tea wouldn't taste right. Or at least, those would be the excuses I'd make as I'd not be able to express why I had to move on, again, stowing the kettle safely amongst my belongings as I did so. I'd claim it was written in the leaves, as I'd try to get my bearings.

Brewing a cup with this kettle makes me know how far away I am from my true north, and helps to sustain me as I make the journey. Sometimes it's alone, but more often than not I'm boiling the pot with water enough for a pot made for sharing.

I'm feeling more settled these days, admittedly, although I find myself still testing new tea leaves and vessels in my search for the perfect brew.

I place the cuppa requested by the locksmith next to him, as he continues to tinker around with faceplates, deadbolts and the right equipment needed to keep the right people in, and the wrong ones out.

He pauses and pauses his work to take a sip (milk, two sugars). 'That's a good cup of tea, that.'

Ten Steps from Home
NOAH BIRKSTED-BREEN — HIGHLY COMMENDED

Lips squeezed to oblivion, he chose to drop the topic altogether after his gravelly neighbour informed him:

'It was Keeley's kids who did it, graffiti-ed the swastika on the grey block where the Orthodox Jewish families live.'

Skirting past the last-standing pub in the area, he'd imagined shouting *Well, hello there!* and explaining to Keeley's pups that it's *not OK* to draw swastikas—suddenly enlightened, like blond stick Buddhas, they'd sniffle and apologise. No, he'd nodded past Keeley and shelved his world-changing plans, slamming the black gate behind him. There'd be other... seasons.

In bed, as his eyes power down for the night, he hears her electric voice ring out across a hundred-metre zone:

'Emelai!'

Without any place to play in the two-bed flat above the pub, the five girls and boy lived on the roads around the pub in the day—only retracted in by rope, by Keeley's voice, sometime before the cut of midnight. Darting behind brick council estates or laughing in the unlit park, this was their home—pub, pavement, park.

'Emelai!'

He pulls the duvet higher, right up to his eyes almost, and wonders: maybe he got it wrong? True, there's an area of brick on the grey housing block, where something's been scrubbed off. How can he be sure? Keeley's a woman who could save a life or end a life. If he's mugged again, he wants her as the onlooker—fag eternally in hand, she'll jump in and nut the guy, maybe kill him with her voice.

'Emelai! Emelai! Emelai!'

His duvet smells of cleaning product, lemony lime. Wouldn't it be great to hang out in the park at night. Sitting on tree trunks near the swings, drinking on moonlit tennis courts! His feet turning to grass. Viewing Earth from the tree tops.

From her breath, he'd not been sure which beverage she'd drunk, but Keeley was leaning too close to his mouth when she'd ambled into his house party a week ago, trilling out her deep worries, they'd found a lump in her breast, how will her little boy cope without her? He'd tried to reassure her, *the tests might turn out negative*? In her metal voice, tempered by ivy:

'All right, love, I'm off for a smoke.'

Relief, he'd felt, relief as she'd tripped outside onto the patio—hopefully back to her flat where Romans and dinosaurs could be running around; sparks, fires and lightning bolts, he always imagines. Sitting on the sofa is her four-year-old, Ricky, forgotten in her fag-dash. *Lucky he knows the roads.* The boy waddled off home after a bit.

Echoes of 'Emelai!' 'ai!' 'ai!' 'ai!' he imagines but night's fully knocked out day. None of the roaring parties that flare up on full-moon Friday nights; no faceless voice from the pavement belting out never-ending, atonal melodies. Into the slipstream of sleep he stumbles. She must be home. Keeley's home, the husband and boy are home, all six kids are home... Emelai's home.

HACKNEY
We Sleep in These Sheets
JARRED MCGINNIS — LEAD WRITER

I keep bringing divorces home, dropping them on our bedspread for her to find. 'What's this?' She asks, more curious than disgusted.

'Remember the lady, the one with the twins.'

'They have curly hair?'

'The twins? Yeah. Kind of weird looking. Like aliens.'

'Cute though.'

'Yeah, cute. Cute aliens.'

'Cute aliens,' she agrees. We both stand and look at it. I become embarrassed at my compulsion to bring these inside the house as if I am beckoning misfortune. At the centre of the bed, it barely makes an indentation.

She asks, 'Do you know what happened?'

'Twins, right? She was always worn out. Three years, no help, no childcare. I only saw the husband on the weekends.' I reach out and lift it by a shattered wing — I think it's a wing — and bring it to the bathroom. The eye is a white blank and the meat is always darker red than you imagine. It takes a couple good flushes. The wreckage of four lives swirls and spins, an Old Testament angel, then it goes down. There is no trace. Not even a smear to remind me.

The next day, I do it again.

'This isn't going to happen to us,' she says.

'Look at it. They were together since they were twenty, like us. They had a ten-year-old boy together.'

'I'm going to have to wash the sheets again,' she says.

I tell her the story, pointing out what I think is a coil of intestine and a shatter of bone. Over the years, they forgot to be a couple. The only thing they did together were things with the kid. They had no shared interests, which at first was bothersome until it wasn't. It eventually didn't matter. They both had busy jobs, but they were at all the recitals together. They were good parents. That felt enough. But it wasn't. Then some woman at his office flirted with him and he flirted back. Actually, I don't know if that is true. His exact words were, 'And I started fucking around.' I'm projecting. I'm trying to communicate something to her. I am hoping she will hear.

'You have to stop doing this.'

I nod because she is right.

I lie beside her. I put my hand on her hip. She's reading her book. I kiss her. No response. It's been a long day for both of us. I should probably go to sleep. Instead, I'm crouching in the garden. A handful of grass comes up like a scalp-hunter's prize. I scratch at the black wetness and the pulsing red veins of worm.

I try not to get dirt on my pyjamas, because she will complain, but it is impossible. I reach inside myself, through my navel, hunting for ours. Its eye searches behind a pink, closed lid. Alive but weak, it nudges at the bottom of the hole. I cover it, patting down the soil, afraid of what might grow here.

HAVERING
That Heart-Break Thing
SHUPAULA MISTRY — WINNER

It wasn't the first time this had happened. Most definitely not. That's what he was told at school. He shook his head and pushed his glasses back up the bridge of his nose. Mother had said not to frown because not only did it keep pushing the frames down but her heart would break if she saw his face like that. Mother's heart often broke. Once it broke when he and his sister were playing in the fields and she fell in some mud and ruined her coat. More recently was yesterday when Father had bid them farewell. Father held his shoulders and declared, 'Olek, you must look after your mother and your sister.' There was that heart-breaking thing in his father's eyes, but Father always managed to keep the water from coming out.

The satchel was heavy on his back as they trudged along the footpaths. It was filled with tins of food, packets of treats Olek was very keen on opening soon, his favourite toy, a fighter plane, and his sister's teddy. The path was becoming increasingly difficult to traverse as they veered further away from the main roads. Mother said that they had to be quick as they could to reach Medkya. After that they could carry on walking or go on a bus. A little pocket radio Mother carried with her kept telling them that their brothers were waiting for them at Medkya and ready to join the fight. Whose brothers were these? Father only has one brother who lives directly two floors below them. Mother has no brothers only two sisters. Olek had asked yesterday about where his brothers were that the man was talking about on the radio. His mother tenderly placed a hand under his chin and said, 'All over the world. They will join us soon.'

Mother suddenly stopped and placed his sister on the ground next to him. She looked scared and gestured to them to go down closer to the ground.

'Who is there?' a voice boomed from the opposite direction. It was hard to see through all the trees.

'Come out, we won't hurt you,' it said again.

Olek's mother looked back at the children. There was that heart-breaking thing again. She turned back and slowly raised her arms and body into a standing position. Her breath could be seen.

'State your business,' the voice was closer this time.

'I am trying to reach Medkya. I am a civilian, you must let me pass.'

'Come forwards,' the voice said curiously.

Mother stepped forwards. Olek held his sister close as he peered through the gaps in the bare branches. The leaves crunched and there was a sound of a scuffle.

'No please, I have my children'. Footsteps came closer and then a shadow appeared over Olek and his sister. This time Olek had that heart-break in his eyes, which the shadow man saw.

'Go home,' he said to Olek before taking his mother away. Home?

HAVERING
Home Improvements
AMANDA WYNNE — HIGHLY COMMENDED

'I remember she had loads of knives sticking out of her though...'
The young woman trailed off, face as red as her scarf. Please don't
think I'm crazy, said her upward gaze.

'Come on! Thought you had a challenge for me,' Gene's voice
boomed over the bookshelves, followed by his elongated blond-
topped head. 'We've got that exact edition. Your pincushion lady is
a still from the film.' He beamed at her. 'It's *Carrie*, by Stephen King.'

The young woman's eyes lit up. She murmured a quick thanks
and hurried away.

'Take out some of his others too,' Gene called after her. 'You're
going to like his stuff.

He rested his elbows on top of the metal bookcase. Head-height
for most, chest-height for him.

He blinked in the low winter sun, magnified through the great
glass wall of the library.

'Gene?'

A bespectacled woman appeared at his side. He turned his
many-toothed smile on her.

'What can I help you with today?'

'It's a lady writer,' she said with pride, adjusting the bangles on
her arm, 'Crime. I can't remember her name, I just know she has
three of them.'

Gene reached, spider-like, all the way over the bookcase to tap
at the shelves on the other side.

'Mary Higgins Clark,' he said warmly.

The woman hurried round to look.

Across the library, a newly arrived gaggle of teens looked uncertainly around the room.

'Far corner.' Gene called over, craning his other arm up and over his shoulder to point awkwardly behind him.

The bespectacled woman whispered, 'What's in the corner?'

'*Twilight,*' said Gene with a pained expression.

'How do you know that's what they're after?'

Gene smiled, 'I'm just that good.'

The teens soon piped down, sinking into the cushions, books in hand.

The library settled into serene sun-kissed page rustling, before an extremely large man with a mobile phone slammed open the door.

He stopped barking into his phone just long enough to instruct the hunched woman behind him to sort printing some documents, then walked over to enjoy the view from the windows.

The woman went straight to the printers, fumbling for her card with unsteady fingers.

'When you're done with that...' She jumped as Gene appeared beside her. 'I'd like to try to tempt you again with this.' He jiggled a DIY book in her peripheral vision.

'I told you, we're not looking to do any home improvements,' she said softly, eyes darting between the printer and her husband's back.

'Check it out, have a flick through,' said Gene. 'Chapter 3, lots of ideas for nice inconspicuous patios.' His gaze flicked to the husband too.

The colour drained from the wife's face.

'Buck up,' said Gene, brandishing a second book. 'You might consider this one too...'

'*Taxes for Dummies*?' She read with a frown.

'Don't forget to buy your birthday lottery ticket next week,' Gene smiled, showing a few too many teeth. 'But if I were you, I'd get that patio sorted first.'

LEWISHAM
The Gathering
RUTH BRADSHAW — WINNER

Even in my bedroom, I can hear the murmur of voices and the occasional clink of glasses rising up from the crowded rooms below. These are such familiar sounds, but I'm not used to hearing them in my own home and I hesitate for a moment on the landing, trying to remember what I came upstairs to look for.

I've dreaded parties since childhood, when Mum insisted on organising huge birthday celebrations for me despite my fear of being the centre of attention. I'd thought Simon shared my views on this and it came as a shock when he first suggested having a party 'to celebrate our quarter-century together and my half-century on this planet.'

Perhaps because we seemed an improbable couple, people quite often asked how we met, and Simon would always take great delight in telling how our eyes had met across a crowded bookstall. He was so unlike anyone I knew back then but I loved the way he said 'absolutely' instead of 'yes' and 'splendid' instead of 'great' and was so sure of his place in the world and of what he wanted to do with his life. I loved that he talked so much about so many things—books, theatre, music, history, art—but never sounded like he was trying to be clever. Most of all, I fell in love with the way his love for me held me tight while still leaving me free to be myself. It didn't smother me in the way Mum's love had always done.

'We talked about how absolutely amazing this house would be for parties when we first looked round. Don't you remember?' Simon said when he next raised the idea. All I remembered of that first viewing nearly a decade ago was my excitement at the prospect of finally being able to grow vegetables. I had always thought that the large south-facing garden was our only reason for buying a house which, as Mum frequently pointed out, was far too big for just the two of us.

Now the house is filled with people and, as I stand at the top of the stairs listening, my emotions spiral between regret for all the opportunities we missed to do this sooner and relief that Mum seems to be on her best behaviour today. I have always avoided introducing her to Simon's parents, knowing how different they are and how embarrassing Mum can be. But earlier I saw her talking quietly to Simon's mother and giving her a gentle hug. I should have realised sooner that there were more important things to worry about.

I glance around anxiously for a moment, still searching for whatever it was I came upstairs for and then I remember. This has happened so many times over the last ten days and each time it hits me anew. It is Simon that is missing.

LEWISHAM
The Alternative Case Note:
'Aluna Moved to a New Foster Placement'
HARRY IRVINE — HIGHLY COMMENDED

We sat side by side, social worker and child, staring out at the road that lay before us. I was giddy with relief that Aluna was actually there in the car, clutching her bag of Cadbury Twirl Bites, fizzing with nerves. I got her to direct me through the traffic-laden roads of South London, trying to occupy her with a practical task. She pointed out the spire of the Crystal Palace transmitting station, telling me she loved to go there at night for views over her city. We turned onto a long sloping road, the door numbers counting down like a stopwatch to our destination, I watched her out of the corner of my eye shrinking down into the neck of her puffer jacket. I wanted to grab her to stop her disappearing, but I felt her slipping down into the black collar like she was being swallowed by a wave.

With the wheels turning to a tacky halt on the hot tarmac road I turned to her. She wouldn't look at me now, staring instead at the melting chocolate in her hands.

'I'm not going to leave you here unless you tell me it's OK.'

She looked at me then and I held her gaze, trying to let her know she would be all right even though I did not know this to be true. When we had arrived at her last placement she had run away as soon as we got out of the car, and I hated that this time she wouldn't try to flee because she knew this was her only option. After a few weeks of staying on the sofas of shadowy unknown adults all over the city, there was now a resignation in her, a silent acceptance that foster care might be the lesser of two evils.

There was an unspoken agreement that we wouldn't call it 'home'.

'It's NOT my home,' Aluna had shouted when we had been at her last foster placement a few weeks earlier. She had balled herself into a duvet cocoon, and the only point at which her heaving sobs quietened was when I told her how much I knew her mum loved her. That was home, the feeling that her mum was with her, even when she couldn't be.

We got out of the car. The heat of the afternoon sun beat down, as if this was any old Friday, as if Aluna might be about to casually ring her cousin's doorbell to while away the rest of the day. The force of her bravery to give this another chance caught in my throat as the passenger door slammed shut. Hope against hope, I willed the knock at the door to be answered by someone who could encircle Aluna with a steadfastness to anchor her in the storm.

She gripped her suitcase and the bag for life crammed with school uniform. 'Can you remember to get my memory box from the last place?' she asked in a small voice.

NEWHAM
A Prison Gets to Be a Friend
JAY A GEE — WINNER

With a start, she wakes. There was a noise, she's sure there was a noise. Scratching, maybe? Glass breaking?

Pulling aside the blackout curtains, she peers out, bloodshot eyes barely emerging over the windowsill.

From above, craning her neck, she sees the grey cotton of a hood in the last gasps of fading sunlight. Head cocked, she tries to decipher muffled voices. There are two of them in her back garden, among tall weeds shooting up between faded paving stones.

Grey-hood is fiddling with the back door. The other, ginger hair sheared off in a crew cut, hops from one foot to the other and peers at the alleyway next to the house and up at the windows.

With a sharp intake of breath, she flings herself back onto the bed. Did he see her? Scrawny and smooth-cheeked, he hadn't looked old enough to drink, let alone break into someone's house.

'Ghost!' local teenagers yell up at her window most days, stones clattering against glass. And, to be fair, she feels like a ghost. Is that why this is happening, they think the house is derelict? Or, worse, they know she's here...

Scrambling off the bed, tired body aching, she crawls along the stained shag carpet to the house phone on a cardboard box. The phone's dial tone demands: *Call the police.*

'You don't understand,' her whisper harsh. 'I *can't.*'

Last time the police came, they'd barged inside. 'You can't barricade yourself in here!' the massive officer had shouted. Grey eyes looking down in disdain, he'd wrinkled his nose at the stench of her fragile body. The psychiatrist with them demanded: 'Come voluntarily or we'll section you.'

'No,' she'd said, over and over: 'No,' till they'd slunk away.

Once, she'd let in a social worker. 'I think I've been here forever,' she'd told the woman. 'I mean, I grew up here, but my family are gone, they all died or escaped—moved out I mean... War of attrition, I guess. I think I went out sometimes when I was a kid, I'm not sure, it feels so long ago. I'm older than I look; lack of sunlight. I mean, I...'

The interloper had looked at the empty room, mould creeping up walls and water dripping down them, and red gashes littering ashen arms, before scurrying away.

After that, she'd stopped answering the phone.

'They put paper through the window once, on fire, but it was mostly smoke and ashes,' she whispers to the phone, breath catching at a clatter downstairs. Tears hot on her cheeks, throat tight she forces out, 'Pages from a dictionary; I think it was meant to be ironic, I think—'

Stairs creak, one, then another. On the floor, she tightens her arm around her calves, bones harsh under threadbare gingham pyjamas.

As a thud rattles the bedroom door, gentle as a knife through butter she replaces the phone in its cradle and the endless tone stops dead.

NEWHAM
The Nice One
MARJORIE BROWNE — HIGHLY COMMENDED

The Phone rings… it rouses me from my deep, pleasant slumber.

I am loath to answer it. I ignore the constant ringing, which feels like a bee buzzing around my ears. I blink, releasing the bread-crumb-like crusts from my heavy-lidded eyes.

I glance at my Apple Watch, it is 4 AM here and it is still dark as sunrise is not until 6.45 AM.

I hear the ringing and wonder for the briefest of moments—is it him?

Something has happened somewhere…

I dreamily scan the moonlit room. I yawn. It is comfortable here, well furnished and… I feel safe. I am 4,075 miles away, on this beautiful remote idyllic island.

The sun will gradually rise and toast my pale, battered English skin, this is where I have escaped to. The Atlantic Ocean laps the shore on one side and the Pacific violently pounds and crashes against the other.

I gingerly answer the phone and emit a croaky 'hello' from my sleep-encrusted mouth.

The Nice One speaks in a quavering, unfamiliar voice. She is trying to be strong but it is obvious she is straining every sinew. Gone is the joy and infectious enthusiasm and the smile you can feel beaming like a vibrant sun-kissed day, warming your heart, through the phone. Everyone referred to her as 'the Nice One'. I even introduce her as 'the Nice One'.

The Nice One lives in East London. She inhabits an average first floor, two-bedroom converted flat with an amazing white-and-red fully fitted, all-singing, all-dancing IKEA kitchen that, surprisingly, has a beautiful black marble floor. Everyone who enters feels they have arrived in a different world, like Alice visiting Wonderland, and cannot believe the transformation.

You enter the flat through a two-feet-square shared communal area littered with old post, various assortment of shoes, an old discarded broken hoover and leaves blown in by the wind off the cracked and dirty pavements. The external door is constantly broken because it is constantly slammed by the numerous tenants from across the globe that the council inflicts upon the ground-floor, uninsulated, damp and vermin-infested flat every six months.

She stays because of the excellent transport links, her wonderful diverse friends, her much-used rainbow-coloured umbrella, her abundant collection of indoor vibrant green, flourishing plants, the giant tree outside her window that scarily raps its branches on the pane in winter when the storm rages, the squirrels that occasionally scramble on the tree/roof, the damn twittering birds, the blasted foxes that keep you awake at night, crying like new-born babes demanding suckling and the diverse restaurants that pop up and disappear regularly. The Nice One loves the community, despite the noise, the fireworks, the overflowing bins, the filth, the homeless begging food or change on a daily basis, the gangs, the mindless youth violence and the sleepless nights.

In the confused haze and muddle of words I hear... Come Home... Come home NOW!

REDBRIDGE
Waiting for God
ANNELIESE AMOAH — WINNER

I thought I could see the motherland through my curtains this morning. In fact, felt it on my face before my eyes registered a portal to the sun. There is a certain kind of peace that arrives with a stream of light. Enters a space quietly. Invites you to remind yourself that *this is a new day.*

There is also a certain kind of rude awakening that will have you regretting opening your eyes too soon. I smelled the ocean's children being bathed in oil downstairs—an incomprehensible time of the day to be carrying out such an activity without the rest of the household's permission.

'YAA!' Mum shouts.

Here we go.

'Yes Mum.' I respond.

'Don't you hear me calling you?'

The whole street can probably hear you.

'Yes Mum.'

'Thursday born but your mind is still in Tuesday. Eh, these children. They will kill me one day. How many times must I call one person? I am certain you will even miss God when he comes back to this earth.'

I could tell by her tone that her frown lines had increased like ruled paper.

'Yes Mum.'

'So, you can't see that there are clothes to be hung?'

I literally just woke up.

'Yes Mum.'

'Laziness will not get you anywhere.'

Well you lay on your back and here I am, so it got you somewhere.
'Yes Mum.'
I go downstairs, still in my pyjamas, bearing features of a moon
that had not seen water and grab the laundry basket.

I often get tired of repetitiveness. Everything feels like a unilateral cycle.

My mother always reminds me how my father is an important
businessman who is very busy. I wonder if she knows that his business involves alcohol and other women. But what's my own? They
will say I am an evil child if I speak.

I step into the jungle that nobody has time to tend to, yet we notice
daily how much the grass is fighting the weeds in reigning length.

Even on a sunny day you can still tell that the London air is carrying the weight of the whole world.

I overhear neighbours shouting about someone letting a cat out.
Smell someone cooking a full English a few doors down. See my
neighbours on the other side of me close their windows like the
British borders. Wishing I could shout, lie in a bed of roses and
shut out the whole world too.

I finish hanging our worries on the line and retreat back inside.

In the same amount of time it took me to do a chore, my mum
still hasn't sat down.

I wonder if she knows that life is more than a bent knee
contorted back
blistered hand
calloused foot
sung hymn
painted smile.

I wonder if, when God does come back to this earth and it's time
to go home, all my mother will say is, 'There are dishes to be washed.'

REDBRIDGE
Like the Turtle
JENNY GIBSON — HIGHLY COMMENDED

I am a loner. Not by choice, by circumstance. Without adequate shelter from the elements, fair-weather friends are left behind. Some journeys you must walk alone. Ours is a city you can get lost in. Yet I am also one of many. Like the pigeons of Trafalgar Square. You throw the likes of me what you have to spare but I cannot live on the fleeting generosity of others.

I am a scavenger. I haunt the streets at night much like the foxes do, barred from the warmth of the indoor world. I look in on the happiness of others, always from a distance. I make sure of what people discard without thought. There are many ways to survive both on the edges of society and the consciousness of humanity.

I am a wordsmith. Though like everything else they sometimes desert me. Words refuse to flow; the well is dry. What is it that you think I am asking when I say, 'Can you spare some change?' Your eyes skitter away like spooked horses. 'No, sorry,' you may mutter. I might as well be asking, 'Can you spare some time?' or 'Can you talk to me and actually hear me?' My story is not so different from yours. Do you care? I suspect your answer could still just as easily be, 'No.'

I am a traveller. Always moving or being moved on. Like a turtle I carry my house with me wherever I go. To you it might look like a ratty old backpack, but I have inside all my previous things. Photos of people I have loved, mementos of a better time. 'Don't you have a home to go to?' you shout at me. I lost it like many things to the fire. Is that what you want to hear? There were no literal flames but there was a burning of more than one bridge. I am homeless, directionless, transient but I have a place to call home, I just carry it on my back.

I am a Londoner. And not just because I was born here. These are my streets. I know them better than many. I know the ones you are unlikely to ever venture down. The ones you avoid. The ones where the unwanted hide. I am as much a part of this city as the statues that watch over us all. Are you scared to look in my direction in case you too are turned to stone? Or is it that you fear that only then will you realise that your heart has already done so. Don't turn away, follow me. Move through our capital like the Thames and see the metropolis as you never have before. Its true nature. I may be an unconventional tour guide, but I guarantee that the sights you see will stay with you. And you'll remember to ask my name as we part ways, so you can return to your city and me to mine.

TOWER HAMLETS
Gummy Bears
ROSALEEN LYNCH — WINNER

We are flesh-eaters, your sister says, and you correct her, meat-eaters, you say, and when you explain that the difference between meat and flesh is that one is food, and the other isn't, she nods in that root-of-a-future-vegetarian way, and the pictures she paints of animals have missing legs, and sometimes lose their heads, and some have bites taken out of them, even dogs, but all the pictures she sticks on the fridge have red puddles or clouds of red raining down, and she creates GIFs at school of Damien Hirst exhibits, of sheep, cows, pigs, three foals looking like unicorns, and a brown bear and zebra, some talking, some just crying red, and you share your gummy bears with her when she stops eating eggs and wait, until she once more refuses roast chicken at the dinner table, to tell her how gelatin is made.

That was when it happened, not the time you're supposed to be watching her and you go off with your friends instead to sneak into the afternoon showing of the latest Bond movie, and she sits on the steps of the porch until you come home, drawing pictures in her composition book and making patterns in the ground with leaves and twigs, and it wasn't the time you left her at the mall, when you wave goodbye, saying you're going home, pretending to leave her there, laughing at her laughing at the joke, waving back, and when you don't come back, though she thinks you took the joke too far, she still thinks it's funny, and draws a comic page to catch the moment, and it wasn't even the time you told her, at your auntie's house, that your parents must have run away from home because they were tired of looking after her, when you knew they were dead, that they drove off the motorway that day on the way to pick her up, when you'd forgotten, and even when your auntie slaps the ham toastie you're raising to your mouth out of your hand, and tells her the truth, hugging her, still your sister gives you one of her cheese-and-onion slices, and though you think that's the day, you don't figure out it's not until you see her first exhibition, called At Home With Family and Other Animals, where, in all her family paintings, you're replaced by a red gummy bear.

TOWER HAMLETS
Maginy
TOM O'BRIEN — HIGHLY COMMENDED

When Dilly checks the sky a third time I call her into the shade. She's got too good at telling time and knows Mags should be long back by now.

I hold out my good arm for her to slide under. She sneaks a look at the slack one and I pretend not to notice. I got chased from the wing bridges and fuselage shanties at Heathrow. Left behind a bucket full of good mussels and the use of my left arm. Now Dilly's mother is back there and I'm sick at what might be happening.

Dilly's skinny frame bumps the metal lean-to. She makes an 'oops' face while clay rattles like thunder for rain that won't come, but doesn't even try to look sorry.

'Tell me a maginy creature, Granda, so I can draw it,' she says, her charcoal stick scratching over faded drawings of things she's never seen.

I search the triangle of blue beyond the tunnel exit sign I live under.

'Draw the body long. Like an eel.'

She'll tire of this game, like her mother did. For now, though, every dig of her bony elbow in my ribs is precious as fresh catch.

'Give it wings, like the gulls we fought when we fished the Strand, remember?' But she's lost in her drawing.

'Next, do a tail. No, not like a rat. Like a fish fin.'

Dilly draws a catfish tail, and I say fine, why not.

If I could only keep her as safe as she thinks she is. For Dilly, this is just how it is. For Mags too, now. It creeps up on you. It's not like they put up signs — Sorry sir, you can't cash your water chits till next week, when the apocalypse starts officially.

What a fucking thing to miss. Planes. My eyes cloud the abandoned sky.

'What will I call it, Granda? I know. I'll put a face on it like an otter or...'

Her chatter tinkles like drops into a rain trap.

I lay my head back and close my eyes. Imagine jet engines drawing white breaths in thin air, the sun flash on a proud tail, wings scoring a shadow cross on the earth.

The last time I saw a plane in the air, I was a boy.

I wait for the contrail to disappear.

Dilly tugs, wanting me to look, but I put my hand on hers, silencing the charcoal rasp.

We listen for the trailing of an empty bucket along what used to be Terminal Road. Dilly's young ears hear it before me, but I'm on my feet and I'm running as fast as I can with her and I don't care how old I am or how broken.

TOWER HAMLETS
The Alderton Farm:
Interview with Claire Spencer
NATASHA BROWN — LEAD WRITER

Claire opened the large front door to her Cobham home one-handed — her left arm was wrapped around a shyly curious toddler. We sat in the kitchen with a pot of fresh mint tea between us. Little Rosie lay on the soft-play mat in the corner, kitted out in stripy leggings, a builder's hard hat and a glittery tutu, mumbling as she forced plastic trucks to collide. 'I'm a designer,' Claire says. Since Rosie's birth in 2018, Claire has taken on part-time freelance work for a handful of clients. Before that, she worked at a boutique branding agency, after studying Art History at university, where she met Richard Spencer. They married soon after graduation, living in London apartments until deciding to move to the suburbs.

Claire is sanguine about the separation, 'People change, don't they?' Their suburban house had never really felt like Spencer's home — 'He stayed in the city most nights. His hours were so long, it made sense.' Spencer had spent weeknights in his Kensington pied-à-terre until Rosie's birth when, increasingly, he began to spend weekends away from his family, too. 'I'm not stupid,' Claire says of the unspoken affairs, 'I know what goes on.' Still, it wasn't until Claire found out the extent of Spencer's involvement with a younger colleague that she decided to officially call it quits. 'There's a line,' she says. Spencer had crossed it.

A few years earlier, Spencer had bought the Alderton farm — an old hill-top property in Kingsford, a quiet West Yorkshire village. Claire didn't think much of the place. 'It's a complete wreck.' She doesn't mince her words. 'A rubbish-heap on a big hill in an awful little town.'

Claire's dismissal of the farm hit personally. I grew up in Kingsford, a stone's throw from the Alderton farm. I walked past it almost daily as a child, even spending occasional summer afternoons 'mucking in' with the Alderton family. Fresh produce was a staple at our dinner table. Nothing at the supermarket can beat the warm, frothy taste of unpasteurised cow's milk, ladled fresh from the milking bucket. Though economically disadvantaged, and unapologetically working class, the town provided a wonderful backdrop for my childhood. It has value. But somehow, our country's towns and industries became the playthings of London's elite.

The Alderton farm fell onto hard times in the wake of the 2008 financial crisis, when the government subsidies that buoyed the farm's modest revenues dried up. The Aldertons searched for new owners who would continue to run a community-minded farm, but eventually sold to property developers. No investment or redevelopment in the area took place, however, though the farm changed hands a few more times. The abandoned plot became a familiar pockmark atop the town's hill. Until, in 2016, Spencer snapped up the property at auction.

'He has a weird prepper fantasy. He thought he could survive the end of the world there or something.' Claire is doubtful, 'I've never seen him do so much as water the garden.' Spencer went on to renovate the farmhouse, fashioning a luxe refuge for when society inevitably collapsed — possibly galvanised by his part in the '08 crash, and the societal fragility it revealed. But when global catastrophe did arrive by way of a novel coronavirus, Spencer clung to London's familiar comforts: restaurant deliveries, his housekeeper, and fibre-optic broadband speeds. He remained at his home, in Kensington. And the Alderton farm stood empty.

WALTHAM FOREST
Accommodating
SAM BURT — WINNER

DISCREET_NOW asked me 'do u accom', which meant 'can I orgasm at your place, where my family/housemates/partner/children won't hear me?' I said yes because I didn't have any of those—*can't* have them, for involved reasons—and because, despite our differences, we both wanted the same thing: someone to help us feel normal for an hour.

To flick a switch on

and off again.

But that's not what happened. *DISCREET_NOW* rolled over and fell asleep. In the morning I said, 'Let yourself out,' and in the evening he was still there, eating curry horizontally. He didn't respond to my questions. He seemed to be sleepwalking. He looked happy.

It wasn't so hard having him around: just another mouth to feed, another set of clothes to wash. But he grew familiar. I missed seeing myself through a stranger's eyes, which I only got to feel by inviting them into my home. I knew where this would lead, and it did.

To me, a week later, lugging home eight cereal bowls from Poundland.

It stopped at ten. For a while. Then it went up to twelve. It kept going up, while the dimensions of my modest flat—designed for two people and a cat at most—remained the same.

The kitchen became a production line, and basic household maintenance my second full-time job. Two bunk beds appeared— from who knows where—and the rest slept everywhere: on and under tables, in the bath, on the kitchen worktop. Several hammocks criss-crossed the living room. My floor was carpeted with interlocking male shapes.

Fuck_now. Quick Meets. I lost count of them. *EasyGoing. Eyeballs, Aubergine.* I lost track of time. At some point, the flat developed its own microclimate. Clouds of steam and Lynx deodorant simmered under the ceiling. I lay awake on the windowsill watching rays of morning light pass through them into green-purple-gold. It always rained after the orgies.

I only wanted things to go further and faster, so that the relief when it was over would be that much greater. I was squeezing in a lifetime's worth of accommodation, so that I could become the island I had always wanted to be.

I couldn't justify perching on the windowsill any longer; it took up too much space. In the middle of the night I fell into a sea of dozing bodies, and it swallowed me whole.

It held me there, suspended an inch below the surface of wakefulness, dreaming dreams that did not seem fully my own but felt guest-written, perhaps by the men whose thighs and torsos warmed me through on all sides. I hadn't known that warmth could reach that far into a person, or that if you held someone close for long enough, you could forget where you finished and they started.

The next morning, they were gone. A note on the table—whose hand, I don't know—said *thanks for everything.*

A week on, the flat looks presentable again. Any day now, I expect to feel relieved.

WALTHAM FOREST
After
CHRISTINA CARÈ — HIGHLY COMMENDED

When he goes, she'll be different, my mother tells me. Can sixty years of marriage be erased with a death?

We can hope, Mother says.

I will find Nonna seated on the lounge, needles in hand, yarn gathered by her slippers. 'Hello figlia,' she will say, trying not to stare at my tattoos.

He's the one who's dying. But I place myself by her side, watch her fingers turn colours over. Transform neat links into rows of flowers.

I visit, one of the few. Hopeful parties have come and gone, the cousins, second cousins, nephews, nieces, looking for a slice. Swarmed around his chair, they listened a while—his knees sore, feet swollen, chest aching. We shooed them, citing Covid, his medicine hour, a scheduled doctor's visit.

One cousin said, 'God she's difficult. He *is* dying.'

This because she had begun to argue. Her version of history vs his. Didn't care who might hear, had it out right there and then, as he tried on his truth.

The cousins take his side, of course they do.

They don't know it's because of the letter he wrote four years ago, that time he threatened to end it all early. In it, he called her a whore. Those words are written.

So, she argued. Five foot nothing and ready to fight.

But not today. Today she has her place on the lounge, him in his chair. He begins to snore. I ask about her roses.

Come, she says. Let's look at them.

It's a slow journey down the hall. Where others once tread, now swept beneath that Persian runner, the walls lined with her handiwork.

Tapestries of knights and princesses, of putti mid-laughter. They watch as we pass the cabinet that housed his rifles; empty now. The little table by the door with the black rotary phone.

Outside, admiring magenta petals, she says: Can you imagine? If he died in there?

I can imagine—she fears the after. Can you argue with a ghost? She would have to leave.

From this hard-won home, its fireplace ablaze even in a mild autumn. From the crucifix in broken clay above the door.

Three generations in our family, she tells me when she catches me looking. Then the frown; before *he* broke it.

He, who spent every cent on cards and horses. Who called her a whore.

We return to the chair, his snores, passing by the 'good' sitting room that awaits everyone's visit. The day the family is reunited at the table. Perhaps that day is coming soon now.

By his side, she changes the subject: Coffee? Biscuits? Bread? A fresh peach?

No, I don't require anything. Just her weighted breathing and the crickets singing in the roof. I want to tell her she can stay forever. But I can't keep the promise.

I can promise I'll return.

And someday, take that letter. Folded and kept in the drawer of that little table, by the door. Beneath the phone that no one calls.

WALTHAM FOREST
All Her Tomorrows
IQBAL HUSSAIN — EMERGING WRITER

'Be brave, my girl,' says Ammi, stroking my hair. 'You will be home before many summers have passed.'

We both know this is a lie. He has mentioned several times how dear the flights are.

'Think of the life you will have there. You will live like a maharani.'
Another lie.

*

As the aeroplane lifts off, I am convinced it will fall apart. I clutch His arm and feel Him tense.

He leans back and closes His eyes. His pale skin, straight nose and pomegranate-red lips remind me of another. Despite everything, I find myself smiling. Except this man could be his father. I remove my hand from His arm.

I spend the rest of the flight with my own eyes shut, picturing the mountains, fields and rivers I am leaving further and further behind.

*

'Let me do the talking,' He says in his formal Urdu as we walk to the counter.

The English man asks me something. I shield my face with my dupatta.

'She eighteen,' He answers on my behalf. 'She no speak English.'

The man inspects my passport, comparing the picture to what he sees before him. Once more, he asks me something.

Once more, I am denied my voice: 'She my wife. She living England now.'

The man calls someone else over. I put my head down, but they indicate that I show my face. I lower my dupatta and my eyes. How will I explain to Ammi if they send me back?

Finally, they stamp the page. A nod and a wave and my kismet is sealed.

*

'Welcome to your new home.'

He sweeps His arms before the red house as though it were a mansion. It squats in a long row of similar houses. There are no mountains or trees; no sunshine, just a sky the colour of cobwebs. As my teeth chatter, I pull my sparkly cardigan tighter. He gifted it to me under Ammi's approving gaze. How can something so beautiful be so inadequate?

Inside, it is dark. He flicks a switch—the bare bulb buzzes into life like an angry makki. Instead of the whoosh-whoosh-whoosh of the ceiling fan, there are just the muted cries of children playing outside. I shiver again. He will want a family, but I do not know how. Ammi did not tell me.

I barely take in the furniture of my new life: a settee propped up on books; a mirror festooned with peacock feathers; two mismatched chairs around a Taj Mahal dining table. He proudly shows off a gold tiger on the mantelpiece.

It is not enough. My heart pounds in my ears and I stifle the sobs that threaten to erupt.

'Forgive me.' He drapes His coat over my shoulders. This time it is my turn to flinch.

My steps falter. He reaches out, but I am elsewhere: adrift in a coracle on the ocean, bobbing and spinning, turning and lurching. A giant wave surges towards me.

Breathe.

Breathe.

Breathe.

I will not go under.

WALTHAM FOREST

█████

RUTH GOLDSMITH — EMERGING WRITER

The crack and split and greed and tear and waste and want of war eats them out of house and ████.

War has come to their front door, an angry man, a shouting screaming cursing man, a hungry man they can't ignore. War makes himself at ████.

The house is no longer a ████ but a carcass, no longer where the heart is. They pick up their skin and bones alone and start the slow march down the longest road they've ever known. The slowest way round is the shortest way ████—but it's nameless now they are ████less.

Crossing land is hard. Then they reach the sea.

To stand on the beach in the dark, to trust a promise of safe passage, to hear the water suck and beckon, is to sit atop the crest of a wave between faith and madness.

But what choice do they have? There's no place like ████, not any more.

So they redefine what a ████ is. Seven months in, the tent on a hillside in the mud and the crowd and the cold and the noise and the thirst and the stink is a ████ of sorts, a place they call ████

at least, a broken kind of ████ where warmth is a metaphor and people are the bricks and mortar.

They stand twice more on beaches in the dark, hearing water suck and beckon, hope in pixels on a tiny screen, until they reach the country where a man's ████ is his castle. They all look like castles from the outside, too.

They try to live a life. They try to build a ████.

But here, they learn that some words say and sound the same but the meanings we give them are different. Some words we read in quiet and tidy ████s in our green and pleasant land, over breakfast, a head shake, pass the jam.

STEALING ████S AND JOBS

Some words we scroll through on phones that never run out of charge, distracting ourselves on the bus, a flick, the story's gone.

CHARITY BEGINS AT ████

Standing by those same words on the news rack, in the shop, they wonder what they did that was so wrong.

GO BACK ████

GO BACK ████

GO BACK ████

GO BACK

One day, the letter comes to say this place is not their ████. Removal vans will come, it says, for them, not for their things.

The toddler plays with her building bricks on the floor, as they turn the words over, the words that turn their world over. This is the only ██████ she's ever known in the only country she's ever seen. How can she be returned somewhere she's never been?

When the vans arrive on the street outside, they spill ██████ Office branded men. And once again, to their front door comes a man, an angry man they can't ignore, a man who won't tell a house from a ██████.

Instead he says: open up.

We're coming in.

It's the law.

There's no place like ██████.

Not any more.

South London

BROMLEY
Alice Tarleton: The Only Man at Zumba
Elaine Wedlock: From Battersea with Love

CROYDON
Elizabeth Uter: This Is Us
Sayyara Nurmahomed: No Place Like Home

KINGSTON UPON THAMES
Chris Williams: Moving On
Heather Mathew: Home

MERTON
Lui Sit: Australian Made
Steven Moe: My Voice

SUTTON
Miranda Lewis: The Last Place
Becky Bone: South of the River Above the Clouds
                in the Night Sky

WANDSWORTH
Rizwan Piracha: Sticks and Stones
Helena Michalacopoulos: Arteries of the Home

BROMLEY
The Only Man at Zumba
ALICE TARLETON— WINNER

On three sides of him ladies—they're always ladies—limber up, shiny Lycra stretching, sweetshop colours below muted T-shirts. Robert—they only know he's Robert from the register—stands by the air conditioner, hugging a carrier bag, the kind you used to pay 5p for before everything became bags for life. His jogging bottoms look soft, but elastic puckers over the belly.

It's Claudia's class and when she enters with a cheery 'Hello!' the rumble of chatter dissolves. Everyone faces her, ears of wheat turning to the breeze. Two new people today, no injuries. Has anyone put the air con on? A false start of feedback noise then the drumbeat kicks in, a syncopated rhythm that takes everyone (except Claudia) a few beats to get in step to.

They move up and down, united in concentration. Left to right then left again. Robert watches the woman—lady—diagonally in front of him. The sinews on her neck pulse and flex as her feet move, once then twice then one, two, three. Robert is a step behind, then two. He shuffles closer and closer to the air con.

He must stand out, the only man at Zumba, the only one not in those tight shiny leggings, but no one acts as though they notice him. He takes a floral water bottle with a scuffed lilac lid out of the plastic bag and cradles it with both hands.

Next it's 'Stayin' Alive', though not the version he knows, there's a man growling over the top about getting raw with the people on the dance floor. Robert stretches, reaches, taking his lead from the diagonal woman but really he's treading water, gulping for air. If he closes his eyes he could be John Travolta, but in the giant mirror he sees a greying man swaying, suspended between fluorescent strip lights and the basketball court markings on the floor.

On the walk home he hums and shimmies from side to side, but he can never remember the steps on his own. He takes off his trainers then tips the water bottle up on the draining board, traces a thumb over the dent on the bottom where Ellen once wrote her name.

He doesn't try to stop himself thinking of her, never does after Zumba. He wonders if she stood near the air con, knew how to work it. Did she giggle trying to cha-cha? He'd only ever thought to ask her a vague question or two each time she got home, his eyes still on the movements on the TV screen.

He puts on 'Stayin' Alive', the original, the one they used to dance to sometimes when she was still well enough. After a verse he is pressing pause and searching again, overriding it with the version from two hours earlier. And now in their home he remembers not just El, but also his class and being in the room without her but with all those potential new acquaintances, and dancing again.

BROMLEY
From Battersea with Love
ELAINE WEDLOCK — HIGHLY COMMENDED

He's been here again. I know it. I can sense him, I can smell him. He's been in MY HOME!

I know what it's like to have no home. The streets are cold and cruel. Danger lurks at every corner for someone like me. I always managed to find somewhere to shelter but sometimes people didn't want me there. Ok, some people were kind, giving me some gentle words and attention, the odd meal here and there. But I felt so alone in the world and it wasn't home.

Then those people came and took me off the streets. They treated me with care and dignity. They gave me a room of my own and a warm bed, three meals a day and sometimes they would visit with me and stay a while. I enjoyed their company. I thought that might just be enough for me. I liked to watch the trains go by from my window, the light twinkling off the river, boats bobbing on the river's tide and gulls swooping and squawking through the air. It was cosy, but ultimately that cost me my freedom. I was stuck in that room without the freedom to roam as I wished.

Then a new chance at life came along. Moving from the tiny South London room to a house in the suburbs. A beautiful garden full of new sights and smells to experience, the ability to come and go as I please. I now have my own family. I am loved, I have freedom and security.

Then he turned up. Sniffing around my home, my family, my things and her. Why does she let him in, why doesn't she just chase him away, tell him he's not wanted, that she doesn't need him. She has me now and we are happy. But he is there, and I never know when he will turn up, where he comes from or why she doesn't turn him away.

So I get scared. I don't want to go back to the tiny room on the river, or the cold wet streets of South London. I make a plan. I have to scare him off. I wait up all night, watching, waiting by the door. If he dares step foot into my home I will show him who's boss.

She wakes up early, sensing that I am not by her side, wondering where I could be. She searches through the house, calling out my name. Finding me at the kitchen door, too scared to go out in case he is there, but determined to defend my territory if he dares to step inside my home.

'Don't worry, Ziggy,' she purrs. 'Everything is going to be all right. You live here now, I brought you home from Battersea to be loved. I know you don't like other cats. I will get you a new cat flap that only opens for you, then Timmy from next door will never bother you in your own home again.'

CROYDON
This Is Us
ELIZABETH UTER — WINNER

This is our city, our house, but it's on the edge. More like country—squirrels, foxes, snooping birds, gossiping about *that family*. Almost a Disney, technicolour wonder, an adventure like a Persian rug ready for flying, it has fringes, each knotted drop of string reminding us we are present, correct, alive, together. Squeezing past each other. Brother farting, shouting 'Roadblocks' he certainly did.

So much fun seeping into our skins not so much through touch or hugs but just being seen, allowed to be. It was not a *children should be seen and not heard* family. We were loud, gave as good as we got, until gone.

We lived on the edge with a wood fusing into the back garden like milk joining coffee. We could see deer, my dad would lick his lips, '*I'm going to catch one, you watch me.*' My eyes would widen, '*No, leave Bambi alone.*' My knowing brother retorting, '*They belong to the Queen, they're wild, she'll have you, if you take one.*' In the end, Dad never did get one. He bought goats instead. He thought he was back in Jamaica, returned one day with seven! Lucky the garden lay on the city's edge, lush green bush into back woods. We worried they were for eating. Dad's smile wobbled, '*Oh no, they're for pets.*' I grouched. '*Pests you mean.*' Greta, the leader of the pack, ate my green designer jumper when on the line. I'd bought it from my first wage packet. Obviously thought it was hanging grass, ready to eat, I could have...

This house hanging on the snaggle-tooth edge of the city had night-time visits from fat badgers like armed gangsters, muscling in to steal from our bin. Black-and-white shadows seen from midnight windows. Rolling rubbish everywhere, guess who cleaned up their mess?

Dad on Sundays. After Mum prepared a roast that sunk your belly, we had to wash up. Maybe, I'd clean dishes, maybe, my brother dried, we'd both put away. Dad with tea towel on shoulder nodded, watched then slipped away but we were so absorbed with *mild clean fairy liquid* bubbling in the sink, slopping to the floor because my hands were slapping bubbles, push them over the edge—we didn't realise he'd left. This happened every time, finally, we'd look at each other, roll our eyes then swivel them towards the crash of music, thundering through doors, all the way to the sitting room. We'd peep in to watch Dad twisting to Motown tunes, Elvis Presley, or Dolly Parton, take your pick. We'd see him lost in moves, our hands to mouth, and laugh. He'd turn his head, wink, close his eyes, fall deep into the vibes.

Mum, tired after the epic preparation, would rest, feet up, in the depths of her bedroom catching up with letters, books, calls to Nana.

This was our house over the years, us against the world. All of us together, until much later, we weren't.

CROYDON
No Place Like Home
SAYYARA NURMAHOMED — HIGHLY COMMENDED

Through crimson autumn leaves, Mya walked briskly from home to school. Dreaming of eating her delicious eggy bread with a drizzle of honey, sweet strawberries sprinkled with cinnamon.

Like robots on a conveyor belt on the road, she inevitably arrived at school to experience the reality of a blasting bell and a blackboard that suffocated her imagination and daydreaming irritatingly well. Playtime was the best time; Mya, Sabrina and Timothy would enjoy games of hopscotch, diligent observers of their special observatory, the playground. The commotion of where they ran free for fifteen minutes seemed a lifetime, compared to the repetitiveness of lessons, lunchtime, home time and bedtime.

At last, back to the aroma of uncut sweet apple and sliced bitter oranges, this was standard practice at home. It was Mya's mum's ritual to keep their palate clean.

It was a full house: Mya, her sister, mum and two uncles from abroad. Her mum doted on her uncles like sons she never had… Her father worked to provide, so they could survive. He would whizz through the door just in time for the six o'clock news and a decadent dinner with succulent pieces of his favourite meat diced by the local butcher, father's friend for life.

An air of loneliness without her father made Mya miserable gradually. Mya's uncle took time to notice and talk to her, learn her behaviour, watch her sweet soul play her favourite games. He took time to connect and create memories, and he promised to always be there. He would listen, comfort and cuddle Mya into a happy trance. Mya felt full of multi-coloured butterflies fluttering. Instead of seeing red, she ate her dinner and went to bed.

119

Tucked up safe, Mya never saw the devil in his chase, how he would creep in, his breathing slowing against her face. Initially her heart burst, a cuddle to tuck her in. This wasn't a sin. Until her heart thundered and cried a multitude of silent tears of terrible fears, she realised he mesmerised her with lies, whilst laid paralysed. Her chords couldn't move to scream, she couldn't push or move out of reach. Her eyes glared into an abyss of neglect, she became the subject of his vulgar hunger, a new project.

Quiet as a mouse, she prayed God would save her. With his power, without a word, he broke her to devour her blooming flower. Child to a woman in an instant. The sickness in her stomach was frozen as he caressed trying to tantalise, kissing and pressing; her heart bled the colour purple. Her brain numbed, thighs collapsed, he invaded shores and crevasses of her innocent island. Before claiming victory, a bomb detonated. The explosion of her sister falling out of bed ended his siege of her territory, forcing him to retreat behind enemy lines.

The lesson she learnt, when a trigger's pulled by a perpetrator, trust, loyalty, love and safety are shot dead. Mya would never be whole at home again.

Moving On
CHRIS WILLIAMS — WINNER

Piles of your possessions cover the floor. It looks chaotic to me, the cables, screens, so many plugs. I watch as you scan the floor. I can see only random items. I can't categorise them in my mind, but there's no need, because they mean something to you. It's organised, you assure me, and as you point out the groups of items—these to sell, these to take with you, those to give away—I can see the logic, the workings of your mind.

I know how to play it too. Listen to your plan, go along with your instructions, tossing in an idea here or a thought there. We're on the level, working together, but it's your show. It would be different with Dad here and we both know it. It would become Dad's show and we'd be bit-part players. But this is one of many steps in your great adventure. Giving notice at work and to the letting agency. What's the rush? Checking the Schengen zone restrictions? Why not play it safe, get a contract in the UK first? Opinions. Advice. All well-meant. But you know your own mind and I know to trust in that.

Here, today, it's calm, it's fun. I can feel your strength of character in your decisiveness and bow to your methods. You suggest a way of sorting a mass of small items into a box and a carrier bag. The stuff to keep goes in the box, the stuff to throw away goes into the carrier bag to be sorted downstairs into recycling, paper and landfill. I would sort it straight into those categories as we go. Dad would do it differently again. But the time spent debating it would fuel resentment and alter the mood. You're the lead in this production.

We laugh as we drop something. We giggle as we move that screen for the third time—Dad would be creating by now—and I make some coffee to reward us both, but really you, for your approach as you embark on this enormous task of packing up and selling your possessions to prepare for your nomadic life.

The zest for clearing out anything superfluous to living your life is contagious, and I am mentally gearing up to following your lead with my own clutter at home. We live so differently, you and I. You eschew my trappings, even my fridge-magnet photos of us all at Legoland, preferring a minimalist environment. Out go any symbols of your childhood and school days. It hurts. Your new life beckons; you're putting your past in its place.

I joke that, one day, you'll have fridge-magnet photos of your own, that there's no escape. I can see you thinking. You capitulate on some things and eventually a dozen boxes line a wall of your old bedroom, ready for when you settle into a place that you will finally call home.

KINGSTON UPON THAMES
Home
HEATHER MATHEW—HIGHLY COMMENDED

Mum loves Banjo Man. Her fingers tap and flutter in her lap, like a mist of butterflies rising from her flowered skirt, as the music bobs and weaves around the room. Dad and I sit either side of her wheelchair, facing the patio doors to the garden beyond.

'Did you bring any chocolates?' says Mum. A sunflower gently nods in the summer breeze, and a robin hops and tugs at the earth below. I can see Reg and Diana on a bench framed by wisteria. She leans towards him, a silent communion of comfort as their heads incline.

'Lucky you didn't come yesterday,' says mum. 'We were in America.'

Dad looks confused and starts to correct her, but I jump in and ask her about the trip. Off we go on a journey up the Orinoco, parrots flapping, the thrash of a crocodile tail, the towering walls of the Panama Canal rising around us. Dad shakes his head and looks utterly lost in the reality we are presenting. He picks at a tissue, agitated and disconsolate.

The resident cat jumps down from a nearby chair and eases into a pool of sunlight, as if it's a hot tub.

'Are you enjoying it?' asks Banjo Man, and Mum smiles with the soft beauty of a renaissance Madonna. I think of the photos of their wedding day sixty years ago, Mum's cat's eyes glasses and hand-span waist, Dad coiffured and shiny by her side.

'You cow,' shouts Hannah, and the moment is broken, as a fight erupts over a *Daily Mail*. Mum laughs and tells me not to worry. Staff intervene, and the tea trolley begins its rattling progress around the conservatory. Dad refuses a biscuit, but Mum wants both, and I go to help her.

Mary sees her chance and strides across the room towards my father calling, 'Frank darling, I knew you would come. Shall we dance?' She perches herself on the arm of Dad's chair and begins to stroke his hair. Dad looks embarrassed, but is too polite to say anything, and stares into his teacup.

'I am here against my will,' says Mary. Dad lifts his head and looks as if he recognises her.

A flare path of candles heralds the arrival of a heavily frosted cake, brought in with great fanfare by the cook and set in front of Dad. We all look at each other as an enthusiastic chorus of 'Happy Birthday' rings out, and Dad is invited to cut the cake and make a wish. It's not Dad's birthday for another three months, and we don't know what to say. I quietly tell the cook and the party moves on. By now Dad has shredded the tissue, and a blossom of white confetti surrounds his chair.

'When can we go home?' he asks me, and Mum answers: 'Don't be so ridiculous John. This is our home.'

The cat gets up, his paws padding a trail of white petals, as he walks through the open door.

MERTON
Australian Made
LUI SIT — WINNER

It's the small things. The words *Australian made* on the discounted hand soap in TK Maxx poke an ache inside. I break open the
sealed lid, pull down my mask and inhale the synthesised eucalyptus fragrance deep into my nostrils. I sniff so hard, my head spins.

It doesn't smell anything like the sharp, gummy scented oil that
releases when you crush a dry eucalyptus leaf in your palm under
the fierce West Australian sun. But it scratches an itch of the past
which clings like fumes, accumulating in volume with each passing
day the Australian border keeps me out.

The shop assistant alongside gives me a look. Is it a dirty look?
I can't tell because of his mask. I screw the lid back on and he looks
away. I clutch the dark green bottle to my chest, hugging it in place
of all the people I cannot.

Moving on, the ragtag collection of discounted clothing spread
out before me. Riffling through the endless racks, each item indi-
cates their brand origins are far from this London retail home they
have ended up in.

I'm far from my origins too. First an expat, then a dual citizen and
now part of an unwilling diaspora of Australians scattered around
the world. Our communal rejection by the country's border policy
means we cannot get our inexpensive Tim Tams or stock up on
Bonds underwear during trips back to the big brown land. Despite
being *Australian made*, we cannot meet our maker. We now have
to eat Penguin bars and shop for knickers at M&S. It's not hardship. But it is a reminder of our exclusion. Scratch that. Penguin
bars are a hardship.

Every day is a letting go. I have let go of the eucalyptus. I have let go of the immediacy of old friends; the sun biting deep into my bones. The ageing faces of Mum and Dad, their scent once familiar. I have let go of emotional citizenship to the country that raised me. Each day peels another strip of Australia from me, taking away the certainty of the past. Much like the bark peeling from Australian eucalyptus trees, my identity is husking. Under the unforgiving lighting scheme in TK Maxx, the only certainty here is that the *Australian made* hand soap, a bargain at £1.99, is coming home with me.

MERTON
My Voice
STEVEN MOE — HIGHLY COMMENDED

It's 4.57 AM and I am awake. I start my day, the same day I have been living for twenty-two years. After putting on my fluorescent yellow and reflective grey jumpsuit, I step onto the concrete slabs paving from my council flat to Merton High Street. I reach the bus stop where the 219 bus rescues me from the drizzle. I recognise the driver, Maurice, who grunts acknowledgement.

Exiting the bus at Tooting Broadway, I take the small blue notepad labelled *Wrong-uns!* from my front pocket. I flip through the pages while crossing the street towards Halifax. I reach the Maurice page and place a scratch next to the seventeen already there. Continuing towards the back alley, I collect my cleaning cart chained to the waste pipe.

My route takes me up Garrett Lane. A continuous zing of taillights is interrupted by the gush of freezing liquid followed by a thump to the head. 'Looooooser!' emanates from the passing black BMW. Frozen like a statue being shat on, the smell of sugary syrup wafts up my nose as I grab a rag to clean my face. I take out the notebook and write *DK54 ABB.*

I turn left onto Wimbledon Road, where people keep to themselves and put their rubbish in bins. That changed, though, in spring 2020. With the lockdown, the foot traffic increased, and I could not clean for a while. Everyone got fed up with full bins and just threw things where they liked. When I came back, people came to the cart, for the first time ever, to drop their rubbish and mouthed *thank you* through their masks.

Coming up the Blackshaw Road now, along with the Lambeth Cemetery. My Anne is buried there. Her ashes entombed in the large brick col… col… columbarium outside the cemetery church. I go to see her every day, rubbing my index finger over the stamped brass indentations of *Anne Wilson 1950–2000*. I kiss the plaque and pull out a rag even though no amount of polishing will bring her back.

I am at the St George's entrance now. Over the years, I have been part of a turf war with Freddy Smith, a hospital cleaner. I see his puny frame, spiked grey hair and beady eyes staring at me, waiting for me to step out of line. He's in the *Wrong-un* book, let me tell you.

I head back for Tooting Broadway station, bag everything up, and chuck it in the council dumpster. I catch the bus back, 57 this time, going past my home stop, deciding to visit SW19 Cafe.

'Hi John, how's the streets? Take a seat.' Rose flashes a wry smile, her eyebrows direct me to the corner table. The menu provides my eyes a distraction from Rose's auburn grey hair and curvy yellow chequered uniform. She reaches over to give me my cuppa.

'Hi, Ro-Ro-Rose. How's your da-da-day?' It's 5.18 PM, awake for over twelve hours, and for the first time today, I find my voice.

SUTTON
The Last Place
MIRANDA LEWIS — WINNER

My lookout is here, in a thicket of brambles. It is an ideal refuge, at the very centre of this green plateau, beneath a cloud-washed sky.

Somehow along a quiet track I left behind the main road, the death swish of traffic, and reached fields and a farm that clings to the edge of the city. On the far horizon the sun catches towers of glass and metal where I know I would find concrete and tarmac, few hiding places and food from bins that was sometimes plenty and sometimes scarce. Here I feast on mice from the hedgerows and fat worms from the rich soil, which I supplement with a recently acquired taste for root vegetables from the compost heap—oozing and half-rotted, but then my teeth aren't what they used to be. I look out towards a bed of pink-veined beetroot leaves, a wood-clad barn, a nodding row of artichoke heads gone to downy seed. In the distance a cluster of saplings sheds coppery leaves into a pond. I give the dark water a wide berth but it might, one spring day, bring forth a fine meal of frogs.

Today, I patrolled the perimeter of my new home and a team of humans clearing lettuces leaned on rake and spade and watched as I followed the curve of the hedgerow, before returning to the protection of my thorny cover.

'A vixen,' one said. 'See the white tip to her tail.'

And her greying back, they might have added, her rotten teeth and broken claws. But they'll not bother me here. I am old now and know it in the weakness of my jaw, the stiffness of my limbs and an ache when I rest that feels like something squirming deep inside and eating me from within. But the coat is still thick enough, my tail still fine.

I have known overgrown gardens and manicured parks, a ditch beside a busy lane down to a stinking dump. One sweltering summer we dug a fine earth beside a railway track, a deep cavern rocked by the vibrations of passing trains, and filled it with the suck and squeal of cubs. I have known the scent of blood and milk, the richness of root and earth; a full belly and the gnawing of hunger. I have known the nudge and lick, the pulse and heat, of family.

But here I am alone.

The days grow shorter and the afternoon sky lies pink over the far city. It suits me to have the shadows for company, but the cold is coming. The frost will settle and the mice dig down deeper. The earth will harden and hide her harvest of worms. But there is comfort too in darkness and maybe midnights full of stars.

In spring when they uncover the beds for planting the humans may greet me again, or they may wonder where the vixen with the white-tipped tail has gone. They will not find my bones.

SUTTON
**South of the River Above the Clouds
in the Night Sky**
BECKY BONE — HIGHLY COMMENDED

The weirdest thing happened to me the other night. I was driving back from Tasha's in Streatham: down the High Road, past the Odeon, past the huge Tesco's, through Norbury, speed bump, lights, speed bump, lights. I could drive this route with conjunctivitis. As I approached Mitcham Common, midnight chewed me up. That's not the weird thing but you feel the shift from life-filled houses, Just-Eat takeaways and all-night offies to empty lamp post-lit outskirts, where on one side cement mixers tower over an industrial estate like security guards on a night shift, and on the other there's space, London green space. That space has a golf course. I don't know much about golf but it's probably not a top one, and when I was a kid my best mate's dad would drive us there in his grey Volvo that smelled of Golden Virginia and Magic Trees with 'Sultans of Swing' playing, and we'd watch him practise his swing and putt balls in those tiny holes. So I'm driving past the green space and the atmosphere turns bulky. Sound swaddled like I was holding my breath under water. Nothing seemed real. No other human in sight to confirm my existence. My hand gripped the steering wheel, my foot pressed the A, I pushed the B checking I was in control, down went the C, third gear, driving on, over the tramlines, along the desolate road I've known my whole life, but my destination unknown. A small in-cline, I'd never noticed that. A hill? No. I was in the air, passing lamp posts shining on the road below with white lines blurring into one. I drifted over the park where mammoth roamed and above the manor where Tudors lived, where Henry visited and fucked Anne. South of the river above the clouds in the night sky eye spied the fairy lights of London in my rear-view mirror. I looked ahead. It was clear why I was up there. Levitating in front of me, perfectly spherical with an alluring buoyancy, I was driving towards the moon. She confirmed my existence. She'd done this before—once, after an argument, I saw her from my window and three minutes later I was in the same car driving to the top of a hill to get the best view. But this was different. Flooring the A, I felt like Sandy and Danny waving goodbye to the gang singing *we'll always be together.* We loved that film, my brother and I, *a hickey from Kenickie is like a hallmark card.* A seven-year-old Pink Lady and a nine-year-old T-Bird wanting to be high school kids so bad, but those kids were nearly thirty in real life and what a let-down high school was when we got there. Oh Hollywood. But this could've been a film, or a headline: *Woman in her thirties drives to the moon!*

WANDSWORTH
Sticks and Stones
RIZWAN PIRACHA — WINNER

Perfection! A perfectly symmetrical... How would one describe the shape of a tie knot? Rhombus? Parallelogram? In his youth Mr Mirza had described it, as had all his classmates, as a samosa. He shuddered at the thought. He held the immaculate Windsor knot between middle finger and thumb and raised it till it nestled comfortably inside his collar. He appraised his handiwork in the mirror. Trapezium? Yes, possibly. He made a mental note to look it up as he dragged a comb through his neatly parted snow-white hair. Finally he smoothed down an imaginary bump on the front of his waistcoat and he was ready. The forecast had predicted a fine autumn day with a hint of winter chill in the air. He decided to forego the privilege of free bus travel and walk to the post office.

At first he wasn't sure he'd heard the words correctly, despite the indecorous volume at which they'd been spoken. He was on his way home from the post office and two young men had yelled at him from across the street, suggesting that he 'go home'. The words would have seemed redundant, ridiculous even, had it not been for their tone. And the fact that they'd been accompanied by other words. Words Mr Mirza hadn't heard in many years. Words he'd assumed were extinct but it now appeared they'd merely lain dormant. They'd even, it seemed, gained potency from their slumber. With the blood rushing to his face he fixed his gaze on the pavement ahead of him and quickened his pace.

Mr Mirza didn't want to go home till he'd gathered his thoughts. He saw the entrance to the library up ahead. What was it he'd wanted to look up? *Trapezium*, that was it. He went straight to the reference section and selected a large hardback dictionary.

He stood by the shelf and flipped through the pages. Past A, B and C... past P and Q... past T... His attention refused to focus on the words. He saw instead a million cryptic symbols, opaque and vaguely threatening. He felt no desire to decipher them. No desire to look up whatever it was he'd come here to look up. He turned to a random page midway through the dictionary. He held the book up with one hand, the open pages facing the ceiling. He splayed his fingers to support the weight of all those words. It brought to mind a monstrous Venus flytrap. He snapped it shut with such force the sound reverberated around the room like a gunshot. A man reading a newspaper looked up and frowned. Mr Mirza returned his stare and the man lowered his eyes. An old lady clutching a mystery in her withered hands smiled and nodded, as if in greeting. Mr Mirza tried to return her smile but his facial muscles ignored his command. He returned the book to the shelf, quietly left the library and walked the rest of the way home.

Arteries of the Home
HELENA MICHALACOPOULOS — HIGHLY COMMENDED

'The kitchen is the heart of the home,' Grandma always says. She sits on the wooden chair, her face crinkled like tissue paper and equally full of hidden surprises. Stories burst out of her like blossoming flowers, usually in the warm kitchen.

Her childhood seaside memories make me scrunch my toes, wincing as if on sticky sand. Her tales bring the sharp smell of seaweed and the bite of salt spray. She relives clothes twisting and sticking on wet skin. 'When you tried to change under a towel, there was always a gale!' She laughed like a rusty swing. More often she repeats, 'The kitchen is the heart of the home' as she sits, smelling of gingernuts and tea. The warmth of the Aga drapes around me like a bathrobe, in contrast to her windswept coastal upbringing. However, I do not agree about the kitchen.

I think of our home more as a series of arteries. The idea of a heart is too dramatic to be part of any single room. Our lives flow through the house. I once met my sister winding red wool round the newel post, threading it down the hallway to a living-room chair. 'Tigger tangled it,' she muttered, eyes narrowed, daring me to mock. Yarn crisscrossed the house like a wartime map. I imagined it summarising all our movements: hurrying down for cups of tea, zigzagging to find lost mobiles, purses, single shoes or rushing back for umbrellas. All the time we would have been chatting. So many spoken words, but what of the words we imagined but never dared articulate? I imagined these thought-words turning pale and fading out, vanishing like aeroplane trails above our house.

I said as much to my sister. 'You talk all the time,' she teased, poking at my tummy. 'What could you have left to say?' 'It's not that,'

I tried to explain. 'There is just so much we don't know. Grandma tells the same stories but what about everything she leaves out? It's like those messages in bottles we used to send. We wrote our names and where we lived. If anyone had found them that wouldn't have told them much. Sometimes talking to her is like reading words traced in sand. You don't know who wrote them or why.' Grandma's memory was like the sea. Anything could be brought in on the tide from far below, but she held her secrets tight.

The elderly lady is asleep again. On her lap, Tigger is round as a cottage loaf, nose pressed into her elbow. He always absorbs her scent the way flowers seem to absorb the smell of sunshine and of local rain. The cat splits his time carefully between us all. Soon he will slideoff to jump on me or Mum. He brings something of Grandma with him like a bee spreading pollen. His silent paws pad the hidden arteries of our home. Arteries like underground streams, carrying stories out to sea.

West London

BRENT
Kate Elliott: Home Comfort
Amer Anwar: Return

EALING
Rebecca Dyer: Turning the Page
Sofia A. Koutlaki: Where the Hand Is

HAMMERSMITH AND FULHAM
Sandra Anlin: London Underground August 1962
Suze Lord: The Expat Brat

HARROW
Joan Pollack: My Home

HILLINGDON
Rekha Wadhwani: Home is Where the Heart Is
David O'Sullivan: A Tale of One City

HOUNSLOW
Megan McIntyre: The House of Paper
Joanna Samuels: Home—1975

RICHMOND UPON THAMES
Roly Grant: Dust
Ana Santi: Figures

BRENT
Home Comfort
KATE ELLIOTT — WINNER

A chilly winter's night surprisingly made warmer by a decrepit old house at the end of a winding road. It would have looked impressive in its day. As you peep inside the lower windows, you see candles flickering and a welcoming, crackling fireplace. The flames burst with warmth and energy and the elderly man rubs his hands as he sits nearby. Always too close but this is cosiness that gives him a feeling like no other. Simply enjoying the peace and quiet. From the old battered armchair, his fingers run across the spines of books stacked high nearby. Hardly ever handled and rarely read. Notes they need dusting.

He fondly thinks of the woman who will be downstairs now, probably polishing cutlery while pots and pans bubble away. He imagines the smell of what will be served up that evening but perhaps it is the smoky aroma from the fire that he inhales. Never physically far apart from each other yet having to maintain distance. Open with each other but otherwise concealed. He contemplates how their lives have taken different paths while time has marched on.

In her own world of thoughts and dreams, the woman bustles away below stairs checking the contents of cellar and pantry. Warmed by the oven, this is pure happiness for her in among the fresh foods, fine glass and dull scrubbing brushes. Surrounded by well thumbed, floury recipes. Protecting her delicate clothing whilst rejoicing in the hubbub.

Unexpectedly there is a loud rap at the front door and from the upper level, he groans under his breath. He doesn't want strangers to be invading his home, his space, not today. His creaking joints ache as he eases himself out of the chair. His bones crack like the wood in the grate. Off he totters to reach the door before the knocking comes again. He doesn't want this additional noise in his home. That wouldn't do. He straightens his hair and adjusts his waistcoat and apron.

As he opens the door wide with a pleasant but non-committal smile, he greets Lord and Lady Cavendish. After asking them to wait in the drawing room, he hastens down to the Lady of the House in the basement. He imagines her tidying her hair and clothing in swift movements as she tears herself away from the snug surroundings. She will emerge as the commanding lady, owner, organiser of this imposing but perishing residence. He will serve drinks.

As he announces the arrival of her visitors, his mind drifts back to the gradual reversal of their roles. Neither can quite remember when their responsibilities changed and their love of life soared. It was just for fun at first but when it became a natural fit, there was no going back. It's extraordinary how you can feel better in someone else's skin even if only for fleeting moments. He would say that it feels like being at home with yourself and this brings a wry smile to his face.

BRENT
Return
AMER ANWAR — LEAD WRITER

2017

There was no one to meet Zaq so he took the bus. The sun dazzled him, its staccato glare reflecting from the puddles lining the road as the vehicle sped along. He had been lucky with the weather; it had poured the last few days but this morning the sun had broken through the oppressive grey clouds, brightening everything, transforming the world from monochrome to Technicolour, offering a sense of hope, maybe even new beginnings. He got off the bus in Bicester and walked to the station north of the town centre. There, he handed in the form he'd been given in exchange for a rail ticket then waited on the platform for his train to London.

It was weird, to be there on his own. It should have been the most normal thing in the world, taking a train, something he'd done many times before and yet it felt strange and new. He had over an hour to wait, the later train being cheaper. Thoughts crowded his head, too numerous and fleeting for him to grasp any single one and consider it fully.

He had been away for a long time and had mixed feelings about returning. Things had changed—not so much the places or people he would see again, though many of them would inevitably be different, but rather things had changed with him—and maybe nothing would ever be the same as it had been before. He wished he had some music to lose himself in.

His train arrived and he got on. It was afternoon now, off-peak, and there were plenty of free seats. He sat by the window and watched the countryside whizz past, his own thoughts superimposed on the blur of green fields and blue sky. It wasn't a long journey, about an hour with just two stops on the way. The landscape gradually became more built up: rural to suburban to urban. The train terminated at Marylebone. He joined the throng of people leaving the train, savouring the experience.

Through the barriers, he went to the ticket counter and handed over another form, this time receiving an off-peak Travelcard for it. He went down to the Tube and hopped onto the Bakerloo line, two stops to Paddington. The main concourse here was familiar territory, a place he knew well, once part of his daily commute. He scanned the departures boards for the next Reading service and went to the stated platform. A multitude of butterflies fluttered within him.

The train out through West London was where he really noticed the changes, the remembered mixed with the new. One stop at Ealing Broadway and then it was his. He stepped off the train and was greeted by a sign in both English and Punjabi—SOUTHALL. He felt his heart swell and a tear or two threaten. Idiot, he chided himself.

Up the stairs, out of the station and he was back where he belonged.

After five years in prison, he was finally home.

EALING
Turning the Page
REBECCA DYER — WINNER

'I think it's time we left London.'

Seven words, typed so casually into his messaging app. Words that would once have horrified me.

I looked up from my phone and through the grease-smeared window as the bus wound its way round Piccadilly. If I squinted past the surface squalor and tourist tat, I could just about still see this city through the hungry eyes of the child I once was, back when it first imprinted itself on me.

London had loomed so large then, the centre of the universe. So this was where life was lived, where things happened, where stories began.

Moving to New Cross was a culture shock after my sleepy suburban upbringing, transported overnight from a town where everyone looked the same to a jostling, juddering jigsaw, every Tube carriage humming with a thousand dialects, every street a canvas of anonymous faces—the whole world in microcosm. Piecing it together seemed like a lifetime's work.

Two decades and four boroughs later, I admit this city hasn't always been kind to me. At times it's been downright brutal. London does not suffer fools and God knows I've been one. Yet, like an abused partner unable to escape its grasp, I've stood by it, unwavering and unswayed, until now.

All those rotten flats, filled with mice and damp and holes in the walls that let the cold air bite through. All those cider-fuelled nights out with supposed friends for life, dancing till dawn, and the creeping terror of the long walk home from the night bus. All those gigs and pubs and parties and clubs—the detritus of city-living crashing daily around my ears, the cacophony of life being lived.

But I'd be lying if I said its grip hadn't loosened over time. Not all at once, but in tiny increments, bit by bit—as is the way when one falls out of love—I began to sense the outer edges of what had once seemed boundless.

Maybe it was when my friends began leaving, one by one, sneaking out to the suburbs or other cities far away, starting families, buying cars, moving on.

Maybe I was just getting too old—something I swore would never happen but could no longer deny as those rush-hour crushes made me yearn for space in which to breathe.

Or maybe it was him. Maybe it was the hard-won, long-resisted truth that home is something that lives inside you and not the other way around. That home lives within his arms, within his words and between our sheets—not in the buildings and bustle beyond. That we could be anywhere together, on the other side of the world even, and I would still feel this sense of warmth and belonging, tethered at last.

That a story can begin with a person as much as with a place.

Turning back to my phone, I began to type.

'Maybe it's time we did.'

EALING
Where the Hand Is
SOFIA A. KOUTLAKI — HIGHLY COMMENDED

Long before London became home, it had been an idea in my head.

Grandma was hanging out the laundry in the rear balcony of the Athens block of flats, my first home. An aeroplane crossed the small turquoise tile of Attic sky among the tall blocks of flats.

'Wave hello to Uncle Manos,' she said. The plane was bound for London, the magical place where uncle worked in a shipping company headquarters. Every time he visited, our flat was enveloped in the smell of Embassy cigarettes and the fresh fragrance of a laundry powder that smelled like something out of this world. It was the smell of London: an elsewhere, magical place.

After one of my first English lessons in Year 4, I skipped all the way home waving a spelling test with 'excellent' in my teacher's red flowery handwriting. At eighteen, London took a definite shape and started living between the onion-skin pages of the *Norton Anthology of English Literature*, in the language of Virginia Woolf and E. M. Forster. I was still in Athens, studying English Literature.

Five years later I arrived in London with a battered suitcase full of books and winter clothes, and lodged at Hughes Parry Hall, Cartwright Gardens, London WC1. Room 118 in the student halls was like all the others: bed, desk, fitted wardrobe—but they were not mine. I put down the suitcase in the bare room and opened the only window: the air smelled of open horizons and refuse bins. I took out the London guide map and went off to trace the places where Virginia Woolf and E. M. Forster had lived and walked.

The sun was out. My twenty-three-year life experience in Greece confirmed the Greek proverb, 'you can tell a good time from its morning'. I walked towards Gordon Square, got into a red phone box, and rang home. I wanted to tell them about my flight from Gatwick, the taxi ride from Victoria that passed in front of Buckingham Palace, the separate hot and cold taps in the wash basin that I was unsure how to use. Baba answered. *We already miss you*—CLICK. Already spent, the £1 coin did not even give me enough time to say, *Me too.* I put the phone down and stared at a card with an image of a blonde, semi-naked woman with watermelon-sized breasts. I had no more change. I finally let myself cry—I was miles away from home, alone for the first time. I retraced my steps. The sun had disappeared, and it was drizzling. By the time I got home—the student halls I mean—it was pouring down. The first of many old certainties was demolished.

In time, London became home; it breathed the language that became mine. Home is now where the heart meets the left hand, and they cruise together along the blank paper, sketching the places and the people that populate the homes—past and present—that have been mine.

HAMMERSMITH AND FULHAM
London Underground August 1962
SANDRA ANLIN — WINNER

A Brother's coming up.

I'm going down. Taking home the smells of the night's toil. The woman below turns to me. She steps down. Holds her nose. Disgusted.

He notices me. Must be a daytime worker. I wonder where. He looks fresh. His face matt.

Which island. Maybe he's Trinidadian. This heat is oppressive down here so early. The British tell us we like it hot.

I'm the same time six days a week. Some same faces. Must be his first day. Monday morning fresh as a daisy. So English, am I. By the end of his day he will be shiny like me.

In this sea of whiteness, we bob up to the surface. Meet each other's eyes. We lock eyes. Knowing eyes. Beaches and blue skies and…

Almost here.

In rhythm we nod.

In rhythm we turn. Calypso rhythms. We laugh. Unashamed.

And I say, 'Yeah Man! Wait! Wait! I'm coming up!'

The Expat Brat
SUZE LORD — HIGHLY COMMENDED

The memories she had of home shuffled through her brain like her nan shuffling a pack of cards, with the flip, flip, flip of colours flashing by as she watched. That was one of the memories actually; Nan sat in her lounge in Nunhead, at the foldaway baize card table, cup of Nescafé at her elbow, the smell and hiss of the gas fire in the background.

When one of Nan's rare presents arrived in the post some sultry, festive day—chocolate, melted on the long journey perhaps, or an inappropriately heavy summer dress—she tore off the wrapping paper and breathed deeply, just to be reminded of the smell of Nan's house.

Other memories were less clear and prompted by Mum, but she'd guarded them preciously in all their years abroad: Her best friend Loulou's feet in pink shiny patent dressing-up shoes, summer afternoons in Loulou's messy garden that smelled a bit of dog poo. She couldn't clearly picture Loulou's face anymore, or bring to mind the sound of her accent when she was surrounded by kids with Australian, Malay and Chinese voices at her international school. She remembered that Rocket lollies were her favourite, but she couldn't summon the taste of the purple bit, when all she had access to were fresh mangoes and papayas.

At the weekend, she played with other sun-crisped children, crusted in sand, on sugar-white beaches. But she remembered Greenwich Park, with the city buildings laid out like a postcard and rolling with friends, down to the bottom of the hill where Mum laid a picnic of sandwiches and crisps. No picnics were held in Borneo, butter melted and crisps went soggy in the humidity. Instead, fragrant curries were conjured out of Tupperware and heated on driftwood fires at the beach.

When it was time for them to go home after years, Mum talked about it incessantly and the neighbours asked what she was looking forward to most, so she answered: Nan and seeing Loulou again and Rocket lollies.

Back at Heathrow, the sky was a grey, heavy blanket just above their heads and she shivered so much that her teeth chattered. Surely this couldn't be home? Her memories had all been warm and sunny, like Borneo was.

Nan met them at the airport, but when enclosed in a hug, she found she couldn't fit under Nan's arm anymore and Nan seemed smaller, more frail.

They went to buy new clothes for school, but they were thick and woolly and made her itch. Shoes were tight to wear after years of flip-flops.

They did visit Loulou's new house in Bexley; she preferred to be called Louise now and wore boots and eyeliner. They sat together on Louise's bed and couldn't think what to say.

As soon as she could, she left to go back to Nan's, where she shuffled her photos and pored over happy times and sun-bronzed friends, far away from the place Mum called home.

HARROW
My Home
JOAN POLLACK — WINNER

It's a springboard to living.

It's where I renew my energies, ground myself, rest and retreat to. I consider it a place from where I'll be made fitter to face new experiences whatever they may be.

Home is not perceived by others, not a house for sale, nor a property. Home is a base, a place for returning to willingly, an environment that can be moulded to what I want. Not necessarily a constant unchanging place, more a slow adaptation to how I feel it to be for just me. I can put my rubber stamp there so that it is recognisable as my home with invisible private secrets and memories embedded there.

It has sentimental attachments—family that has since departed to a more permanent heavenly home. They have left their ghostly presences behind and set up home with me. Recipes taught to provide traces of a past warm home life—cholent bean stew, traditional foods help make my dwelling a home. The essential safe place to rest and recharge well out of danger and hate zones. The returning to at the day's end having missed the place entirely. The relief that brings of coming home to sleep to dream.

I have recently developed more of a sense of belonging and pride in my home I have never experienced apart from my birth home on the other side of the Atlantic. Creativity visits there more often to embed and leave my mark in this territory as I choose. I have the freedom here to express myself.

Where could there ever be another?

HILLINGDON
Home is Where the Heart Is
REKHA WADHWANI — WINNER

'Home is where the heart is,' it is said. But what happens when your heart is not in your home but in another place. A place that you cannot call your own. A place so far away that it is beyond your reach, even though it is only five minutes away by car in this city.

This morning everything changed for Emily. The love of her life, her support system, her only contact during the pandemic had died in hospital. Unable to visit, she cries dry tears. The sobs rack her body as she wanders from room to room, not knowing what to do. Today the busy city, normally abuzz with traffic and people talking into their mobiles, is silent, seemingly mourning with her but not comforting her. Emily looks out her bedroom window overlooking the abandoned park. Her bed beckons her.

The ring of her mobile suddenly jolts her awake. The caller asks why she hasn't answered her phone for three days. Three days? Emily does not know, does not care how these days have passed. She is not family. She has no funeral to arrange, no formalities to complete, no activities to help her come to terms with losing someone. Only anger, regrets and what-if questions which no one can answer live here now.

Three days morph into three weeks. Essential shopping is done online. She has no need or desire to meet anyone, go anywhere, or do anything. There is no longer anyone to be accountable to nor anyone to update her, and no-one to comfort her. She cannot explain her grief or her loneliness to anyone. How can she make anyone understand something she herself does not understand. Six million people live cheek by jowl here and yet Emily is alone and lonely.

Three weeks turn into three months. Tears finally come, scalding her cheeks. The park behind her house starts bursting into colour and the daffodils nod their heads, inviting her to join them in their dance. Still another couple of weeks pass in a haze until Emily is finally ready to go outside. She returns home with a tin of lavender-coloured paint and brushes.

Dragging the furniture into the centre of her sitting room, she has something to do. At the end of the day, exhausted with all this activity, she sits cross-legged on the floor with a tin of soup and bread for company. Tomorrow she must cook something with some taste, she decides. For the moment she drags her duvet around her and falls asleep on the floor.

Eventually, with the painting finished and the furniture re-arranged, Emily looks round and a smile tries to push her lips upward. She goes to the local florist and buys the biggest, most beautiful bunch of flowers that they have.

It is time. Time to bring her shattered, fragile heart with its hidden strength, home.

HILLINGDON
A Tale of One City
DAVID O'SULLIVAN — HIGHLY COMMENDED

*He pleaded as rough hands ploughed him through the throng.
'I just need to get this tape to him.'*
'No dough, no show, son,' came the gruff reply.
*He'd snuck in of course—amazing where a hi-vis and a broom
can get you—but had been spotted as he'd made his way to the
stage, demo tape held aloft like an offering to the rock gods.*
*They reached the edge of the crowd and he was shoved through
a side door, landing in a heap on the Embankment.*
*'Please!' he begged once more as the door slammed shut. It was
over. That was his only shot. He had nowhere else to go. Turning
into the setting sun, he was met with the view of Waterloo Bridge,
a vast concrete spine joining north to south. He saw a way out.
He couldn't believe this was happening to him.*

He couldn't believe this was happening to him, he'd never felt
so alive! The music pounded, the crowd pulsing with the rhythm.
Up here, he was a god! Hard to think that just four months ago he
was busking in Green Park station, exchanging songs for loose
change. Now look, on the bill at Somerset House! His fingers
plucked and pinched the strings, whipping the audience into a frenzy. He was on top of the world! There was a record deal for more
money that he'd ever dreamed of and even talk of breaking America.
All thanks to a chance encounter with a certain Rolling Stone on
his way to the Ritz who liked what he heard. The streets, as they
say, are paved with gold.

The streets, as they say, are paved with gold, but not from where he was standing. He stared at Somerset House from the bridge, its green dome bathed in the dying embers of the day. Turning full circle he took in the sight. To the west was the Palace of Westminster, a cathedral to political might. To the east, the City, steel and glass stalagmites serving as statues to capitalism. So much wealth before him, yet all he wanted was enough to get away from the hostel and start afresh. Somewhere he could sleep without waiting for the creak of the bedroom door, the breath on his neck, the shame afterwards. The summer breeze carried the music to him. The pace was quickening.

The pace was quickening. The crowd were going wild. Those at the front were holding their arms aloft. Was there anything more rock 'n' roll than crowd surfing? The tempo increased yet more. He looked down to the surging mass before him.

He looked down to the surging mass before him. He turned away, unsure if he could go through with it. But then, who would miss him? He was no rock star, just a busker trying like all the rest. His heart pounded. Boom, boom, boom.

Boom, boom, boom. The beat reached fever pitch. It was time.

It was time.

They jumped.

HOUNSLOW
The House of Paper
MEGAN MCINTYRE — WINNER

Faster. Pedal faster. She'd never catch me if I pedalled faster.

I knew my destination; I just had to escape her clutches. My legs whirred and the wheels responded. The Woman grew distant behind me. Freedom at last!

On my way up the hill, my shoe fell off. A size too big; another hand-me-down.

Forget it, I thought, I don't need it. Or maybe I was oblivious. It's hard to recall the exact thoughts of a trike-riding four-year-old fleeing her grandparents' house.

I remember I headed to the park at the end of their suburban street, a mysterious land where pinecones decorated the shaded earth. I suspect I was suffering a frequent bout of Middle Child Syndrome, annoyed at the attention my younger sister was receiving and frustrated by the rules of a game my older one had proclaimed we were playing.

My escape was short-lived. After all, I was a child and what felt like an epic journey to my weary legs was in fact only the length of a street. And the park—where the trees gave way to a large open space frequented by teenagers as the sun set—was no place for a lonely child.

The Woman fetched me, and we returned to the house. It was the first time I remember seeing her out of the kitchen.

The next day, she was out of the kitchen again. I was bundled into her car and driven past the newsagent and the grocer. Past the corner store where I was allowed an ice cream on hot days. Past the train station which whisked workers into the Big City. We ventured further, stretching my world's boundary.

Out of the car, the Woman took my hand. We walked towards a glass building, sparkling in the morning sun like a diamond. She opened its door, and we stepped inside a magical kingdom.

Swathed in its silence, I took in this new place. In one corner, there was a play area filled with trucks and dolls and blackboards. In another, adults nestled in brightly coloured chairs thumbing through newspapers. In between were shelves, stretching taller than me and filled with books standing spine-to-spine.

'It's a house of paper,' I announced.

The Woman, my grandmother, smiled. 'Welcome to the library, dear.'

She enchanted me with its secrets. When I was bigger, I too would lounge in the chairs and flick through newspapers. For now, I could free books from their shelves and take them home, before returning to swap them. That I could do this on repeat thrilled me more than Christmas.

Reading gifted me a never-ending cast of characters, each inviting me to be part of their gang. A gang, a family, that was mine. One where I was no longer the Middle Child.

This place, shared with this woman, became my place. This house of paper, alongside my grandmother, my home.

HOUNSLOW
Home—1975
JOANNA SAMUELS — HIGHLY COMMENDED

Mum had finished her first stint in the kitchen for that morning. The meat was seasoned for that evening's meal. Breakfast had been served—toast and marmalade with a cup of freshly made masala chai. The single-glazed kitchen windows were all steamed up and rivulets of condensation were searching then meandering their way down to the windowsill. Outside was cold and this house only had one paraffin heater for warmth, but that was in the living room. Yet, this kitchen, despite its freezing stone floor with patches of torn, brittle lino, which was desperately, though without success, attempting to look like parquet flooring, always felt cosy and comfortable. The shabby furniture was familiar and that stove was always on. Pots and pans would be simmering away with something spicy throughout the day, with enough food to feed the neighbours' kids on both sides, as well as this hungry family.

Mum shuffled down the hall towards the living room, worn slippers slapping against her tired feet. Two children, girls, aged six and eight, played at the table as Mum entered the room. They were still in their matching, faded red flannel pyjamas, and both had heads of messy bed-hair, still tangled from a night of agitated dreaming. Mum eased herself into her armchair with a sigh and a smile to herself; one job of the day done but so many more yet to do. She turned to the shelf on her right and switched on the radio. Capital FM was their station of choice. Graham Dene's voice burst into the room and the children looked up. As the opening bars of the next tune began to play, Mum clapped her hands. This was their favourite song of the moment. As Minnie Riperton's sweet vocals began, the children jumped down from the table and joined Mum on the armchair, huddling up together. They forgot the chill outside and enjoyed the warmth of this moment, of their togetherness and shared love of the tune. They sang in unison—'Loving you is easy 'cos you're beautiful...'

RICHMOND UPON THAMES
Dust
ROLY GRANT — WINNER

There once was a small house, in an urban street, that people mocked because it didn't have a toilet. This is the house without a loo, estate agents said, standing outside, surveying wonky paving and tufts of grass in seed. They talked about getting keys soon, tracking down the owner, about who should knock it down and start again. Then they would head off somewhere nicer.

It was true the house had seen better days. The one, for example, many springs ago, when a man carried a woman in his arms through the front door. And the morning another man, upended halfway through the window, was laughing and laughing having locked himself out. And the holy night, with lamps low, and a baby in the bathtub. A birthday candle left in the corner of a drawer. A faint ring on the floor from a wet Christmas tree. All the homes that never knew each other.

Then, in a blink, everyone was gone and the house became a joke.

Without people to love it, the house went mad. Its grief was written in measurements of height, in different colours and textures, climbing the kitchen doorframe. Its emptiness was baked into the amber of buttons stuck between floorboards, in the sound of the attic door rattling its catch, in the ghosts of fading receipts. The pipes people had laid had cracked. The rendering they'd sprayed had trapped moisture. The boiler, with no-one left to check it, burned a lonely hour every morning. The house cried a big brown stain on the downstairs ceiling.

But as time passed, the house learned to look after itself. The kitchen bin, un-emptied—banana peel, teabags, the outer leaves of a cabbage and some spit—made something new. The eggs of a fly that had visited the banana peel hatched into maggots, which turned into pupae, and then new flies, all alive and buzzing at once. The house smelled fertile. Spiders, related and not, came alive with the flies. They'd been hanging around, half dead and switched off, waiting for a change in the wind. Moisture was eaten. The house smelled of dust. In the spaces between boards and walls, rats worked. They rubbed grease as they squeezed around brittle pipes. They chewed with metal jaws. The house smelled of gas.

People passing in a fair wind would stop to nose the air. Some peered through the front window. A few calls were made. But no-one cared enough. Sellotape curled. Paint fell like snow. In the bedroom, the toilet (of course there was), sat on fading carpet, seat up, empty of water.

One night strong winds tore down the street, causing a power cut. Inside the house, the box failed to trip and the gas was caught. For a moment, clouds of dust bloomed, the bodies of insects rose and swirled, and the emptiness gasped. Then the house exploded, spraying itself into the night. In streets of darkness, it was the brightest thing.

RICHMOND UPON THAMES
Figures
ANA SANTI — HIGHLY COMMENDED

The new neighbours were American. She could hear them, everyone could, from their fenced gardens, terraced within a row of identical rectangular lawns. The Americans' back garden was parallel to hers, separated by a narrow alleyway. Their arrival brought interest to those blended days, under repeated blue skies. Before long, the Americans drowned out the self-conscious Brits with infectious fun. The drone of incessant home improvements was replaced by splashes from paddling pools, tipsy lunchtime chat, the confidence of topless sunbathing. The Americans befriended their next-door neighbours. Over the fence, the children exchanged toys, the adults rosé. But the alleyway drew a line between them and her.

From the vantage point of her daughter's bedroom window, she could see straight into the Americans' open kitchen. Above it was the bathroom—she almost always looked away—and Apple Guy's office.

On weeknights, Apple Guy sat at his desk, the Mac's logo visible from the back of the monitor, framed by the window. His study was directly opposite the room where she worked. He never closed the curtains. He sometimes forgot to turn on the lights, his blue-rimmed forehead hovering in the dark. She felt most productive when she outlasted Apple Guy at her own desk.

Sunday mornings were her favourite time to watch the Americans. Croissants and crayons, endless coffee. Breakfast spilling into brunch. The two brothers, barefoot in pyjamas, got into arguments—a mild shove, tears—but it was nothing The Mom couldn't solve. Slipping into a squat, she met the eyes of the guilty party, one hand on his shoulder. To the other, she placed an arm over his hunched body. Within minutes, they were playing again. The little sister often sat on her mother's lap, having her hair plaited. The Mom had a glossy, bouncy, ponytail that you imagine all American cheerleaders must have. Even the dog had good hair: a shiny, dark-blonde mane, flattened by constant petting.

By the following spring, the gardens were less populated. People were allowed out, into pubs. One hot afternoon, as she put away her daughter's clothes, something caught her attention. It looked like the Americans' dog, but what she could see was in her garden. A much darker blonde—auburn, really—with hair just as silky. Sunbathing on her lawn, fully stretched, lay a fox.

She crept downstairs to the unlocked back door and gently pushed it. The fox didn't move. She clicked her tongue. Ears pricked, the fox lifted her head—body still languid—and turned. Two pairs of brown eyes locked together. She smiled. The fox held her gaze. She flung open the kitchen door. The fox leapt onto the fence and into the alleyway.

From Apple Guy's office, The Mom was staring down, eyes glinting, mouth forming a perfect 'O'. She returned the look, palms up in disbelief and laughed. They stayed that way for several seconds, smiling at each other, before The Mom held up her hand in a half wave.

About the Contributors

North London
BARNET

WINNER: RUTHIE RAPHAEL
Ruthie Raphael has been resident in the London Borough of Barnet for almost 30 years. She is a professional dog groomer and enjoys writing in her spare time. She uses writing both as a creative pursuit and also for therapeutic benefits. 'Taking the Tablets' is her first story to be published.

HIGHLY COMMENDED: SHEREEN PANDIT
Shereen Pandit trained and practised as a lawyer in her youth but she has spent most of her adult life as a political activist, trade unionist, wife and mother. Writing, like sport, fits in there somewhere. Her short stories have won the odd prize. One won the Booktrust London Award and was performed on stage and on radio in the USA. Some of Shereen's work is on the curricula of European high schools.

ENFIELD

WINNER: PAMELA KANDEKORE
Pamela Kandekore currently teaches in a primary school on a full-time basis. Reading and writing have been her favourite pastimes since she was a child. So, she signed up for library memberships wherever she could. Pamela has an MA in children's literature. She particularly enjoys writing stories for children and short stories.

HIGHLY COMMENDED: LISA HARDY

British Born but 100% Jamaican. Lisa Hardy has a rich and complicated heritage. Now her Dad has passed away, she carries the torch of storyteller and writing gives her an outlet to tap into those stories and the DNA memory of her African ancestors. Lisa loves the Arts—she's a keen gardener, an activist and she is very passionate about community.

HARINGEY

WINNER: AISHA PHOENIX

Aisha Phoenix's speculative fiction collection, *Bat Monkey and Other Stories*, was shortlisted for the 2020 SI Leeds Literary Prize. Her work has appeared in Inkandescent's ~~Mainstream~~ anthology, *Leicester Writers Short Story Prize Anthology Vol. 5*, the *2020 National Flash Fiction Day Anthology Root, Tree, Branch*, *Strange Horizons*, *Litro USA Online* and *The Mechanics' Institute Review Online*. Twitter: @FirebirdN4.

HIGHLY COMMENDED: TERRI-CERES DE ROCHÉ-PUCKERIN

Terri-Ceres de Roché-Puckerin graduated from Goldsmiths University twice—once with a BA in English, and again with an MA in Literature of the Caribbean and its Diasporas. She has lived in North London all her life, and is currently a teacher of English at a North London secondary school.

Central London
CAMDEN

WINNER: EMILY GAYWOOD-JAMES

Emily Gaywood-James lives in North West London with her wife. She grew up in the Midlands and spent time living and working in

France, Spain, Denmark and the USA before returning to the UK around six years ago. In 2021 her work was featured in the *This Is Our Place* anthology. She is currently working on her first novel.

HIGHLY COMMENDED: TINA SANG
Tina Sang is an English student at New College, Oxford. She was born in Michigan and moved to Beijing at the age of eleven. She writes short stories, lyrics, and has attempted two novels. When she's not writing, she's pursuing her other artistic hobbies, such as songwriting, piano playing, and dancing.

EMERGING WRITER: S. NIROSHINI
S. Niroshini received a London Writers Award in the literary fiction category in 2019 and won Third Prize in the Poetry London Prize 2020. Her pamphlet *Darling Girl* was released in 2021.

CITY OF LONDON

WINNER: ELEANOR SUE ZHAO
Eleanor Sue Zhao is a writer and trainee lawyer. She was born in China, and grew up in Edinburgh and Cambridge. Her writing explores, among other things, emotions and relationships through prosaic and poetic dialogue. She recently finished *East of Eden* (Steinbeck), *The Old Man and the Sea* (Hemingway) and *American Originality* (Glück) and welcomes any discussion around those books or recommendations for what to read next!

HIGHLY COMMENDED: VERITY GREAVES
Verity Greaves writes poetry, articles, and stories. She has lived and worked abroad but now lives in the City of London. She works in adult learning, is a qualified City guide and is currently writing a novel set in the square mile.

KENSINGTON AND CHELSEA

WINNER: ALISON CATCHPOLE

Alison moved to London after studying psychology at Oxford University. She trained as a teacher and has worked in many schools in inner London, also spending five years teaching in Brussels, and a decade freelance writing fashion articles for luxury lifestyle magazines in Hong Kong. She lives just off Portobello Road and is currently retraining as a lawyer.

HIGHLY COMMENDED: STAN MOORCROFT

Stan Moorcroft has been writing for as long as he can remember. A full career both in the NHS, and voluntary sector, encompassing addiction, offending and mental health, reduced time for writing. Since retiring he has more time to write. One self-published novel, *Jack*, plus poems and short pieces published. Writing is communication, one reader will do.

ISLINGTON

WINNER: HAZEL BEEVERS

Hazel Beevers is a freelance creative producer, writer, editor and photographer. She co-runs The Literary Platform, and writes fiction in her spare time. She is a mother of one.

HIGHLY COMMENDED: ASHLEY PEGG

Ashley Pegg is a writer and an award-winning filmmaker. He was recently selected for the Faber Academy novel-writing course and his films have screened at festivals worldwide, having previously trained at the National Film and Television School. He is also a visiting lecturer at the University of Westminster.

LAMBETH

WINNER: TRACEY HAMMETT

Tracey Hammett is from Cardiff. Most of her family live in Barry, South Wales, so when she isn't in Brockwell Park she may well be on Barry Island Beach. She has worked as a flavourist's assistant, a prescription pricer and a waitress (and in quite a few other jobs besides). She now works as an English and creative writing tutor and a children's writer.

HIGHLY COMMENDED: KHADIJA BADRI

Khadija is a community engagement worker with a background in migrant, refugee and child rights. Her first love was writing, and she often scribbles down stories in her spare time as a way of processing various different life experiences.

LEAD WRITER: CALEB AZUMAH NELSON

Caleb Azumah Nelson is a twenty-seven-year-old British-Ghanaian writer and photographer living in South East London. His photography has been shortlisted for the Palm Photo Prize and won the People's Choice Prize. His short story, PRAY, was shortlisted for the BBC National Short Story Award 2020. His first novel, OPEN WATER, won the Costa First Novel Award, was shortlisted for Waterstones Book of the Year, and longlisted for the Desmond Elliott Prize and the Gordon Burn Prize. His second novel, SMALL WORLDS, will be published in May 2023.

SOUTHWARK

WINNER: EMMA ROBERTSON

Emma Robertson lives with her husband in Elephant & Castle. She finds time for writing around her full-time role as a dance teacher and has been published in a number of anthologies and literary magazines. She was recently longlisted for the Bath Flash Fiction Award and will appear in their 2022 collection published later this year.

HIGHLY COMMENDED: JENNIFER MCGOWAN

Jennifer McGowan, 29, originally from Watford, now lives and writes in South East London. When she was younger she decided she wanted to be the first female manager of Watford FC, visit every country in the world and earn a living from writing. She's still working on it.

EMERGING WRITER: LIZZIE DAMILOLA BLACKBURN

Lizzie Damilola Blackburn is a British-Nigerian writer, born in Peckham, who wants to tell the stories that she and her friends have longed for but never seen—romcoms 'where Cinderella is Black and no-one bats an eyelid'. In 2019 she won the Literary Consultancy Pen Factor Writing Competition with the early draft of *Yinka, Where is your Huzband?*, which she had been writing alongside juggling her job at Carers UK. She has been at the receiving end of the question in the title of her novel many times, and now lives with her husband in Milton Keynes.

WESTMINSTER

WINNER: LORETTA RAMKISSOON

Loretta Ramkissoon is a writer and linguist from London. She completed a BA in Modern Languages and an MA in Translation Studies. She is currently working on her first novel, which explores mixed-faith and mixed-heritage upbringings. She was longlisted for Penguin Random House's WriteNow 2018, is a London Writers Awardee 2019, and her piece 'Which Floor?' was published in *Common People: An Anthology of Working-Class Writers*.

East London
BARKING AND DAGENHAM

WINNER: SHAHEMA TAFADER
Shahema is an illustrator and graphic designer from Barking, London. She holds three legal degrees and was called to the Bar of England and Wales in 2012. She has had her fiction, poetry and art published by *Write On! Magazine* and *Write On! Extra*, as well as poetry published by *Minnow Literary Magazine*.

HIGHLY COMMENDED: DONNA THOMSON
Donna Thomson is a writer of fiction, and ever so drawn to Victorian and gothic influence. She is currently working on a novel and of recent, has collated her short stories for submission in order to bring them to life. She lives in London, with her cat.

BEXLEY

WINNER: TOYAH PANTON
Toyah Panton (also known as Toyah Demi) is a London-born writer, spoken word poet and poetry performer. Through her writing, Toyah enjoys exploring her inner world and internal conversations of the soul.

HIGHLY COMMENDED: ROBERT BUTLER
Robert Butler has worked for some while as a storyboard artist and illustrator, more recently also making music videos and designing album covers. Previous to that he was a computer programmer. Before that he worked in the fields of environmental conservation and archaeology.

GREENWICH

WINNER: S M SMITH
S M Smith is Parent Support for an inner London primary school. She credits has writing success to the courses attended at The City Literary Institute in London.

HIGHLY COMMENDED: MAUREEN STAPLETON
Maureen Stapleton, a journalist, has written for *The Wall Street Journal*, *The New York Times*, *Radio Times*, *Heat*, and many others. She serves on the management teams for the Greenwich Book Festival and the Comedy Women in Print Prize, and is working on her first novel. As a dual British-American citizen, she is bilingual in hot drinks (coffee and tea).

HACKNEY

WINNER: ERIN NIIMI LONGHURST
Erin Niimi Longhurst is a British/Japanese author living in Hackney. She is the author of *Japonisme* (HarperCollins, 2018), *Omoiyari* (HarperCollins, 2020), and *A Little Book of Japanese Contentments* (Chronicle Books, 2018). Her written work is influenced by her dual heritage, and she also works as a Social Media Manager at a cultural organisation.

HIGHLY COMMENDED: NOAH BIRKSTED-BREEN
Noah works at the intersection of the Arts, Humanities and Social Sciences. He runs Sputnik Theatre Company, bringing translated drama to UK audiences. From 2017 to 2020, he was Associate Researcher (University of Oxford). In 2021, Noah completed an MA in Creative Writing at Birkbeck. Publications include *Beef* (The Real Story) and *Snow* (*Hinterland*)—nominated for the Pushcart Prize.

LEAD WRITER: JARRED MCGINNIS

Jarred McGinnis' acclaimed debut novel *The Coward* was published by Canongate (July 2021). It was chosen for the BBC Radio 2 book club and BBC 2's 'Between the Covers' show. Also in 2021, he was chosen by *The Guardian* as one of the UK's ten best emerging writers. He is the co-founder of The Special Relationship, which was chosen for the British Council's International Literature Showcase. He was the creative director for 'Moby-Dick Unabridged', a four-day immersive multimedia reading of Herman Melville's *Moby Dick* at the Southbank Centre, involving hundreds of participants. He also has a PhD in Artificial Intelligence, but mostly he inspires the able-bodied by using public transport and taking his daughters to the playground.

HAVERING

WINNER: SHUPAULA MISTRY

Shupaula Mistry, born in Croydon, was a precocious child of first-generation immigrants. From the age of nine she started writing. Her interests include food, travel, sci fi and fantasy shows and sometimes doing nothing at all. She currently resides in Havering with her husband and two children. Although, her family may argue she actually lives in the library

HIGHLY COMMENDED: AMANDA WYNNE

Havering libraries were a huge part of Amanda's life while she studied at Frances Bardsley and Havering VI Form College. Later Amanda went on to study Archaeology at Cambridge University and University of Reading—working on projects in the US, Poland and Belgium. During the pandemic she moved back to Havering, while working remotely for the British Antarctic Survey in digital communications. Amanda has enjoyed fiction and non-fiction writing her whole life, and is always looking for the nearest library.

LEWISHAM

WINNER: RUTH BRADSHAW
Ruth Bradshaw writes short stories and creative non-fiction and works part-time in environmental policy. Her writing has been published in a number of journals, anthologies and websites including *Reflex Fiction*, *The Clearing* and *Thorn Literary Magazine*. When not writing or working she can often be found in the woods near her home in South London and occasionally on Twitter @ruthc_b

HIGHLY COMMENDED: HARRY IRVINE
Harry grew up in London but moved to Lewisham in 2021 and feels lucky to be part of a welcoming community here. Harry loves this city so much and is delighted to be in an anthology celebrating it.

NEWHAM

WINNER: JAY A GEE
Jay A Gee (they/them) is queer and nonbinary from the distant wilds of Yorkshire. Autistic with multiple sclerosis, Jay is a self-taught writer who escaped to Newham. Shortlisted for: Aesthetica Creative Writing Prize; Creative Future; Penguin Random House's Write Now; The Literary Consultancy's PEN Factor; A. M. Heath's Free Reads Anthology.
Twitter: @writejustincase

HIGHLY COMMENDED: MARJORIE BROWNE
Born in London to parents from Jamaica and Nevis, Marjorie has lived in East London for over 34 years. She is currently Chair of Governors for an outstanding primary school. Marjorie is passionate about Diversity and Inclusion. She enjoys cinema, bingo, axe-throwing and beach volleyball. She also co-sponsors a child in Tanzania. Marjorie loves reading a wide variety of books.

REDBRIDGE

WINNER: ANNELIESE AMOAH
Anneliese Amoah is a 26-year-old British-Ghanaian poet. Her past features and creative engagements include Cece's Speakeasy in collaboration with Apples and Snakes and Spread The Word's #WriteThroughThis anthology. Her work centres around the themes of tradition, family, race and religion.
She can be found on Instagram @awordbya.

HIGHLY COMMENDED: JENNY GIBSON
Jenny Gibson has been writing both poetry and prose for a few years now. She has enjoyed courses in writing and has been included in a few anthologies. She has always loved stories, both hearing and telling them. Her grandmother used to tell her stories when she was a small child and that's where it all started for her.

TOWER HAMLETS

WINNER: ROSALEEN LYNCH
Rosaleen Lynch is an Irish youth and community worker and writer in the East End of London with words in *Craft*, *Smokelong Quarterly*, *Jellyfish Review*, *Ellipsis Zine*, *Mslexia*, *Litro and Fish*, shortlisted by Bath and the Bridport Prize, a winner of the HISSAC Flash Fiction Competition and the Oxford Flash Fiction Prize and can be found on Twitter @quotes_52 and 52Quotes.blogspot.com.

HIGHLY COMMENDED: TOM O'BRIEN

Tom's Novella-in-Flash are *Straw Gods* (Reflex Press), *Homemade Weather* (Retreat West) and *One For The River* (Ad Hoc). His work is Pushcart and Best Microfictions nominated. He's the winner of the 2021 NFFD NZ Best Microfiction and the 2021 Biffy50 Microfiction. He's on Twitter @tomwrote and his website is www.tomobrien.co.uk.

LEAD WRITER: NATASHA BROWN

Natasha Brown is a writer who lives in London. In 2019, she received a London Writers Award in the literary fiction category. *Assembly* is her debut novel.

WALTHAM FOREST

WINNER: SAM BURT

Sam Burt is a former teacher, freelance editor and tutor based in sunny Leyton, where he chairs the East London Indie Book Club. His fiction has appeared in *Popshot Quarterly*, *Bandit Fiction* and *Ink, Sweat and Tears*. In 2022 he plans to launch a new online fiction magazine: pointbloc.wordpress.com

HIGHLY COMMENDED: CHRISTINA CARÈ

Christina Carè is an Italian-Australian writer living in London. After studying Architecture, Art History and Philosophy, she's gone from working on construction sites to interviewing creatives for *Spotlight*, turning data into compelling stories at Google, and writing for the F-Word, Entrepreneur.com, TEDx, among others. Previously a London Writers Awardee (2019) and Faber Academy scholarship winner (2020), she's working on her debut novel represented by Kate Evans at Peters Fraser + Dunlop.

EMERGING WRITER: IQBAL HUSSAIN

Iqbal's short story 'The Boy with the Green Eyes' was published in the *Leicester Writes Short Story* anthology in September 2021. He is one of fifteen emerging writers to feature in the ~~Mainstream~~ anthology by Inkandescent, published July 2021. His short story 'A Home from Home' won Gold prize in the Creative Future Writers' Awards 2019. He is a recipient of the inaugural London Writers Awards 2018 and was shortlisted for the Penguin Random House WriteNow scheme 2017. Iqbal's first novel, *Northern Boy*, is currently out on submission.

EMERGING WRITER: RUTH GOLDSMITH

Born to a librarian and a museum curator, stories were always going to be important to Ruth. In 2019, she received a London Writers Award for Literary Fiction with Spread the Word to develop her novel. Her short fiction has popped up in various places—as a lead on Visual Verse, in the first City of Stories collection and most recently placed first in the streetcake magazine Experimental Writing Prize 2021. As a commissioned writer on the Science Museum's #ScienceFictions project, she's having fun mixing history, science, art and words, with an anthology forthcoming in 2022. Ruth's a card-carrying member of Waltham Forest Library Service.

South London
BROMLEY

WINNER: ALICE TARLETON

Alice Tarleton has worked as a journalist for nearly two decades, including 15 years in TV newsrooms. She is currently focused on raising her young children and spends a lot of time reading picture books over and over again and trying to remember where teddy was last seen. This is her first attempt at writing fiction.

HIGHLY COMMENDED: ELAINE WEDLOCK

Elaine Wedlock is a Mum of two, a Social Researcher in the Ministry of Justice and a mad cat lady. She is an avid reader so she naively thought she could try her hand at creative writing. It turned out to be much harder than she thought but she is going to give it a good go anyway.

CROYDON

WINNER: ELIZABETH UTER

Elizabeth Uter is an award-winning short story writer and poet, winning Brent City Of Stories Competition—2017, 2018 Poem for Slough Competition. She's facilitated Farrago Poetry workshops; Performed at Queen's Park Literary Festival, London. Published: 2019—*Reach/Sarasvati* Magazines, *Bollocks To Brexit* anthology, 2020 *Writing from Inlandia*; 2021, *This Is Our Place* anthology. momentsalongtheway.wordpress.com

HIGHLY COMMENDED: SAYYARA NURMAHOMED

Sayyara works and advocates for young people. Sayyara graduated with an honorary LLB and is a mother of one. Sayyara discovered a passion for poetry, as a means of self expression allowing vulnerability to be heard and seen as a strength. Sayyara started writing later in life through her love for Spoken Word and the Performing Arts.

KINGSTON UPON THAMES

WINNER: CHRIS WILLIAMS

Chris's short stories have appeared in local anthologies and a national woman's magazine, and 'Pulling Strings' currently features in the online CornerHOUSE 'Radio Shorts'. If she's not reading, she's writing, or she's travelling by train and writing about it. A BA in English Literature later on in life formalised earlier locally-run writing classes, and legitimised eavesdropping at any opportunity.

178

HIGHLY COMMENDED: HEATHER MATHEW

Heather grew up in West London and her love of reading and creative writing was nurtured from a young age by her parents, her school and a wonderful local library. Heather has worked in the charity sector for over 25 years, and enjoys living and working in an area rich with green spaces, wonderful arts venues, and the beauty of the River Thames.

MERTON

WINNER: LUI SIT

Lui Sit writes short fiction, memoir, non-fiction and children's middle grade. She is a recipient of the, A Brief Pause, London Writers Award, WriteNow & Megaphone writers' development schemes. Her short stories are published online and in print journals and anthologies. She is also a trained dance anthropologist and cat devotee. She can be found at @Lui_Loowee_Sit

HIGHLY COMMENDED: STEVEN MOE

Steven Moe writes short stories and is working on his first novel. After a 25-year hiatus from creative writing, Steve joined a local writing group composed of parents from his children's school. Steve is an IT professional by day writer by early morning and night. Born in America, Steve has lived in Merton for the last 20 years and loves running, good food, and margaritas.

SUTTON

WINNER: MIRANDA LEWIS

Miranda Lewis is a retired teacher. She grew up in the countryside, but has lived and worked in London for most of her adult life. Miranda is a passionate gardener and enjoys exploring the city's green spaces and hidden corners. Her story is set out in the fields of Sutton Community Farm where she volunteers regularly.

HIGHLY COMMENDED: BECKY BONE

Becky began writing in the form of stand-up and sketch comedy and is an accomplished improviser and interactive theatre performer. She is a recent Birkbeck graduate with a BA in Creative Writing and English, and her poems have been published online and in print with Streetcake, Culture Matters, and Spread The Word.

WANDSWORTH

WINNER: RIZWAN PIRACHA

Rizwan Piracha was born in Streatham but spent much of his youth in Karachi. Despite these early setbacks he went on to become a successful supermarket shelf filler and hospital filing clerk. His short story 'Lateef's Room' appeared in the 2016 Bridport Prize Anthology, sales of which doubled when the contributing authors discovered they'd only get one free copy.

HIGHLY COMMENDED: HELENA MICHALACOPOULOS

Helena is a special needs teacher working with age 18 plus. She has not written stories in a long time but began again during the pandemic. Her cat often strolls into any story she writes as he did in this one. She enjoys living near her family. The workshop she attended was excellent and thank you for running this scheme.

West London
BRENT

WINNER: KATE ELLIOTT

Kate Elliott grew up with a love of reading and the theatre. She lives in London and has worked for Brent Libraries for over 20 years. Kate enjoys attending arts and cultural events. Writing has recently become an interest and 'Home Comfort' is her first published short story.

LEAD WRITER: AMER ANWAR

Amer Anwar grew up in West London. After leaving college he had a variety of jobs, including, warehouse assistant, comic book lettering artist, driver for emergency doctors and chalet rep in the French Alps. He eventually settled into a career as a creative art-worker/graphic designer and spent a decade and a half producing artwork, mainly for the home entertainment industry. He has an MA in Creative Writing from Birkbeck, University of London. His critically acclaimed debut novel, *Brothers in Blood* won the Crime Writers' Association Debut Dagger and was picked by *The Times* and *The Guardian* as one of the books of the year. His second novel, *Stone Cold Trouble*, was longlisted for the CWA Gold Dagger. He is currently working on the next book in the Zaq & Jags series.

EALING

WINNER: REBECCA DYER

Rebecca Dyer was born in Chelmsford, Essex, and has lived in various boroughs of London since 2001. After studying at Goldsmiths University, she began a career as a sub-editor, working for magazines, websites and newspapers. She currently works as a freelance editor and lives in Acton with her partner.

HIGHLY COMMENDED: SOFIA A. KOUTLAKI

Sofia A. Koutlaki's trajectory traced a line through English literature, the Classics, and the interface of language and culture. A life-long observer of Iranians, she wrote about them in her PhD and the book *Among the Iranians* (2010). After fourteen years lecturing in Tehran, she now writes life stories and facilitates online groups (Memoir Writing; Stoic practice)
www.sofiakoutlaki.com

HAMMERSMITH AND FULHAM

WINNER: SANDRA ANLIN
Sandra Anlin is almost a septuagenarian and lives in White City. Since retirement, she has taken creative writing classes and written short stories. Her ambition, however, is to write a novel about the lives and loves of Suffragettes, not just the women but the men, too, who supported the cause and endured forcible feeding.

HIGHLY COMMENDED: SUZE LORD
Suze Lord lives in London now but grew up in Borneo before attending boarding school in the Midlands. She floated around rootless until she had a family and planted them in Sussex. Later, after years of working in Marketing and writing adverts and cosmetic bottle labels, she decided to start putting down on paper hers' and others' experiences, real and imagined.

HARROW

WINNER: JOAN POLLACK
Joan Pollack was born in Toronto, Canada and has been British now for quite a few years. Joan is a second-generation Jew born to 2 holocaust survivors of concentration camps of Nazi Europe in World War 2. She loves creative writing in groups and recommends it to anyone.

HILLINGDON

WINNER: REKHA WADHWANI
Rekha Wadhwani has lived in Hillingdon since 1992 and enjoys arts and craft, including writing. Rekha believes that learning never stops and a member of different groups in the borough and learning from others. Rekha is a coordinator for Project Linus UK

182

making and collecting patchwork quilts and blankets for children, who would benefit from a hug.

HIGHLY COMMENDED: DAVID O'SULLIVAN

Dave is a motor mechanic and budding author. Fixing cars pays his bills, but writing stories makes him happy. And happiness is the cure to everything. He lives in Ruislip, West London with his wife, five children and Buddy the border terrier, who is quite mad.

HOUNSLOW

WINNER: MEGAN MCINTYRE

After completing a BA in English Literature (Melbourne University) and Graduate Diploma in Journalism (La Trobe University), Megan left her native Australia to backpack around North America before arriving in the UK. Brief stints in publishing and freelance travel writing led to her current role in marketing for a range of travel, hospitality and tech companies. She lives in West London with a great view of Heathrow's air traffic, which she tries to not let distract her from working on her writing.

HIGHLY COMMENDED: JOANNA SAMUELS

Joanna Samuels was born and schooled in the borough of Hounslow, and went on to enjoy a career in the theatre and television industries. She achieved her goal of becoming a casting director, working with many inspirational writers and creatives, mostly in comedy. She now works part time alongside being a Mum.

RICHMOND UPON THAMES

WINNER: ROLY GRANT

After studying modern history at Oxford University, Roly Grant worked as a graphic designer, founding a studio in 2006. In 2019 he took a short story writing course at City University of London. 'Dust' is his second piece of short fiction. He lives in East Sheen.

HIGHLY COMMENDED: ANA SANTI

Ana Santi is a journalist, writer and editor. She has written for *The Guardian* and *The Times*, and is the author of *Three Things to Help Heal the Planet*, her non-fiction debut. Ana is the co-editor of *Comfort Zones*, an anthology of women writers, which includes her fictionalised account of growing up in Brazil. 'Figures' is Ana's first short story.

Acknowledgements

City of Stories Home is only possible due to the hard work and continued support of a great number of people. Spread the Word would like to take this opportunity to thank a number of people involved.

Firstly, to the project funders, Arts Council England, Cockayne Grants for the Arts and the London Community Foundation. Without their support City of Stories Home would not possible.

London Libraries for their partnership and fellowship, particularly Caroline Rae for her constant support and belief.

Our partners, the RNIB Reading Services and Libraries Connected for all your passion for the project and support.

The City of Stories Home Library Project Group members, Tim O'Dell, Deborah Peck, Adrienne Tayler, Hannah Richens, Lena Marshall, Deborah Peck and Claire Nicholas-Walker for all your insight, commitment and help in shaping the project.

The fantastic participating library services and staff who were involved in the coordination and delivery of City of Stories Home:

Barking and Dagenham: Lena Smith and Lisa Roullier and all at Barking Learning Centre
Barnet: Catherine Lusted and all at Chipping Barnet Library
Bexley: Susan Prior and all at Bexleyheath Central Library
Brent: Kate Elliot and all at The Library at Willesden Green
Bromley: Jeremy Travers and all at Bromley Central Library

Camden: Nick Durant and Jean Aston and all at
Pancras Square Library
City of London: Helen Tremaine and all at Barbican Library
Croydon: Lucy Lawrence and Rumena Rahman and all at
Croydon Central Library
Ealing: Karen Henry and Martha Lambert and all at
Ealing Central Library
Enfield: Mia MacKinnon and all at Enfield Town Library
Greenwich: Sarah Davis and all at Eltham Centre Library
Hackney: Monica Server and Jon Fortang and all at
Stoke Newington Library
Hammersmith and Fulham: Claire Nicholas Walker and all at
Fulham Library
Haringey: Sara Khan and Elizabeth Cruz and all at
Wood Green Library
Harrow: Matthew Whitewood and all at Greenhill Library
Havering: Kathy Scourfield and all at Hornchurch Library
Hillingdon: Lara Marshall, Bernie McAteer and Darren Deeks and
all at Uxbridge Library
Hounslow: Claire Powell and Hannah Crabtree and all at
Feltham Library
Islington: Tony Brown and all at Islington Central Library
Kensington and Chelsea: Michaela Hope and Clint Sinclair all at
Kensington Central Library
Kingston: Fiona Tarn and Marion Tessier and all at
Kingston Library
Lambeth: Tim O'Dell and Vincia Bennett and all at
Streatham Library
Lewisham: Adrienne Tayler and Jennifer Haynes and all at
Deptford Lounge
Merton: Maria Garcia and all at Colliers Wood Library
Newham: Deborah Peck and Caroline Rae and all at
East Ham Library
Redbridge: Nina Simon and all at Redbridge Central Library

Richmond: Iona Richardson and Jo Withers and all at
Twickenham Library
Southwark: Nell Cooper and Wes White and all at
Canada Water Library
Sutton: Marina Maniadaki and all at Sutton Central Library
Tower Hamlets: Angelina Leatherbrow and Atalanta Kernick and
all at Cubitt Town Library
Waltham Forest: Patrick McGuire and all at Leytonstone Library
Wandsworth: Daniel Andrews and Alex Martin and all at
Balham Library
Westminster: Michaela Hope and Clint Sinclair and all at
Church Street Library

Special mention to Deborah Peck, Tim O'Dell, Karen Henry and
Sarah Ginn from Newham, Lambeth, Ealing and Kingston library
services respectively who all delivered the City of Stories Home
audience development projects engaging communities most
impacted by COVID-19.

The 2022 City of Stories Home commissioned writers Natasha
Brown, Caleb Azumah Nelson, Amer Anwar and Jarred McGinnis.
Thank you producing fantastic stories and encouraging the crea-
tion of many more.

The City of Stories Home emerging writers Iqbal Hussain, S. Niroshini,
Ruth Goldsmith and Lizzie Damilola Blackburn. Thank you for your
amazing stories, commitment to the project and passion for libraries.

The City of Stories Home writer-facilitators: Maame Blue, Tice Cin,
Jemilea Wisdom-Baako, Helen Bowell, Lorraine Brown, Arun Das,
Charlotte Heather, Annie Hayter, Shagufta K Iqbal, Amita Murray,
Carinya Sharples and Chris Simpson. Thank you for your constant
enthusiasm, reliability and for inspiring hundreds of writers across
the city.

Franek Wardyński, for your brilliant book design.

Tasia Graham, for your beautiful City of Stories Home illustrations.

Patricia Ferguson, for your wonderful poster, flyer and book cover designs.

Ana Fletcher, for your fantastic proof-reading and copyediting skills in bringing this book together.

Ronke Lawal, Ariatu PR, for all your amazing work in raising the profile of the project and helping to celebrate our library services.

Bobby Nayyar, Laura Kenwright, Eva Lewin and Emily Ajgan at Spread the Word, for your tireless work bringing this whole project together, and your good humour throughout.

And lastly, to everyone who attended City of Stories Home workshops, everyone who entered the competition and of course particular thanks to the winning and highly commended writers whose wonderful stories make this anthology a reality.

London Libraries

London Libraries is the London region of Libraries Connected and has membership of all 32 boroughs and the City of London. It works collaboratively to promote London's public library network and delivers regional campaigns and annual events such as the London Libraries Festival 'World of Possibilities'.

London has the largest public library network of any major world city. Over 8,000,000 Londoners have access to a network of 325 public libraries. Wherever you are in London you are never far from a public library.

London Libraries supports Libraries Connected's vision regionally to provide an inclusive, modern, sustainable and high quality public library service at the heart of every community. It does this through promoting the value of libraries, brokering partnerships, sharing best practice and driving innovation in the sector

Website: londonlibraries.net
Twitter: @LDNLibraries
Facebook: www.facebook.com/londonlibraries

Spread the Word

Spread the Word is London's literature development agency, a charity and a National Portfolio client of Arts Council England. It is funded to help London's writers make their mark on the page, the screen and in the world and build strategic partnerships to foster a literature ecology which reflects the cultural diversity of contemporary Britain. Spread the Word has a national and international reputation for initiating change making research and development programmes for writers that have equity and social justice at their heart such as, The Complete Works and the London Writers Awards. In 2020 it launched Rethinking 'Diversity' in Publishing by Dr Anamik Saha and Dr Sandra van Lente, Goldsmiths, University of London, in partnership with The Bookseller and Words of Colour.

Website: www.spreadtheword.org.uk
Twitter: @STWevents
Facebook: www.facebook.com/spreadthewordwriters/
Instagram: @spreadthewordwriters

Libraries Connected

Libraries Connected, formerly the Society of Chief Librarians, is a charity and membership organisation that represents public library Heads of Service in England, Wales and Northern Ireland. As an Arts Council England Sector Support Organisation, our mission is to maintain and build on the power of public libraries through our six Universal Offers. These cover the areas of service essential to a 21st-century library service. Our vision is an inclusive, modern, sustainable and high quality public library service at the heart of every community in the UK.

Website: www.librariesconnected.org.uk/
Twitter: @LibsConnected

RNIB Reading Services

RNIB Library is completely free of charge and contains over 35,000 audiobooks and thousands of braille books. Audiobooks are mailed out on CD or memory stick and are also available through Amazon smart speakers using an Alexa skill. Braille books are produced personally for each customer, so readers enjoy brand new braille books printed just for them. And RNIB Reading Services Online Library enables customers to download braille books, which can be read on an electronic braille display, and audiobooks as well. RNIB continuously receives feedback that the Library is a lifeline to customers.

Website: www.rniblibrary.com / readingservices.rnib.org.uk/
Twitter: @RNIBLibrary
Facebook: www.facebook.com/RNIBLibrary/
Instagram: @rnib